In The Blood

In The Blood

Unflinching Book II

Stuart G. Yates

Copyright (C) 2016 Stuart G. Yates
Layout design and Copyright (C) 2020 by Next Chapter
Published 2020 by Gunslinger – A Next Chapter Imprint
Cover art by http://www.thecovercollection.com/
Edited by D.S. Williams
This book is a work of fiction. Names, characters, places, and incidents are the product of the author's imagination or are used fictitiously. Any resemblance to actual events, locales, or persons, living or dead, is purely coincidental.
All rights reserved. No part of this book may be reproduced or transmitted in any form or by any means, electronic or mechanical, including photocopying, recording, or by any information storage and retrieval system, without the author's permission.

Also by Stuart G. Yates

- Unflinching
- Varangian
- Varangian 2 (King of the Norse)
- Burnt Offerings
- Whipped Up
- Splintered Ice
- The Sandman Cometh
- Roadkill
- Tears in the Fabric of Time

Contents

One 1

Two 5

Three 10

Four 14

Five 19

Six 24

Seven 29

Eight 34

Nine 41

Ten 45

Eleven 53

Twelve 58

Thirteen 65

Fourteen 69

Fifteen 73

Sixteen	77
Seventeen	85
Eighteen	94
Nineteen	101
Twenty	107
Twenty one	110
Twenty two	112
Twenty three	119
Twenty four	123
Twenty five	128
Twenty six	137
Twenty seven	141
Twenty eight	143
Twenty nine	148
About the Author	154

One

Utah/Colorado border, 1858

The retort of the gunshots rang out across the still, open countryside, echoing amongst the nearby mountains. There were six shots, even and measured. Simms squinted through the cordite and whistled.

"You've nailed it, Noreen," he said, grinning, and glanced across at the short, dark-haired woman with the striking face, dressed in dungarees and red-checked shirt.

She smiled back at him, cheeks reddening. "Ah, shush, you're just saying that!"

"No I ain't," said the Pinkerton detective and he strode over to the fence not fifteen paces away and looked down at the cluster of tin cans lying on the ground. The holes torn through their sides from Noreen's bullets testified to her improved accuracy with the six-gun. He got down on his haunches and picked a can up, examining it more closely. He straightened his back, holding the can as if it were a prize. "I'm proud of you," he said and nodded across to her. "Reload your piece, Noreen. No point having a gun that ain't loaded." He shook his head, eyes growing distant for a moment. "I've seen that happen more than once."

"What?"

"Dropping an unloaded, just fired revolver into the holster, then dying when another assailant steps up and you ain't got nothing to stop them with."

"That ever happen to you?"

He tilted his head and gave a small chuckle. "I wouldn't be here if it had. Now, reload your piece."

"But I'm so dirty already," she said, giving him that coy look of hers which broke down his defenses with such ease. She held up a hand. "Look at me, covered in all this horrible, black powder."

"Well, that's why I carry three, sometimes more, pre-loaded cylinders." He moved closer to her and for a long time they stood there, so close. After a moment, she reached up and clawed the hair at the back of his head. Melting, he leaned into her and kissed her smooth mouth, the warmth seeping through him.

They pulled apart slightly and he rested his face on her cheek, loving the way her fingertips massaged away at his scalp. Forcing himself back to the real world, he gently took the revolver from her fingers and gave it a long, admiring look. "Brand new, Remington Navy. A fine gun indeed. Easier to maintain than my old Dragoon, that's for sure."

She stared at him. "There's so much I don't know about you. Your life, where you're from."

Simms shrugged. "Not much to tell, really. Maybe when we're old and grey, I'll fill out the long evenings with my story."

"You think we will grow old together?"

"Would you like us to?"

A smile flickered across her full lips, those lips he loved to kiss. "I'd like nothing more."

Now it was his turn to smile, before he lifted the still-smoking gun. "Best take this over to the firing table and reload, like I said."

As he wandered over to replace the cans, he craned his neck to watch her dutifully filling up the cylinders with black powder before ramming home the lead shots with the under-barrel lever. He gave an appreciative nod, settled the cans back on the fence post and moved towards where she stood at the little trestle table. He was about to place his hand on her slim shoulder when something caught his eye. Drawing in a breath, he looked beyond her and peered out across the plain, taking in every detail of the slowly approaching rider. Without a word, Simms took the gun from her fingers and slipped it into his own, empty holster.

She frowned. "I only did four."

"Get inside," he said quietly.

"What do you mean? I thought we might try it again, make sure none of it was—"

"Get inside. Take my carbine from above the door, lie on your belly the way I taught you, and don't make another sound."

Their eyes met and he saw the alarm there. He brushed his fingers across her cheek, to reassure her. "What is it?" she asked.

"Just do it."

With no further explanation needed, she broke into a run, hurrying across to the small, log cabin where they lived together. From above the inside door-frame she pulled down the carbine, checked it, then lay down, following his instructions to the letter.

Satisfied, Simms turned and waited for the rider to come closer.

The stranger sat astride a piebald horse on a brightly polished saddle of coal black. Big across the chest, his long hair fell to his shoulders, hat pushed back to hang down over his back, suspended by a leather cord around his throat. Across his back, a long-barreled musket hung in a frilled canvas scabbard. As he drew closer and reined in his horse, his coat fell open to reveal two ivory handled Navy Colts, butts inwards for a double cross-belly draw. Snorting, the horse pawed at the ground and the rider leaned forward and grinned, his teeth stained brown with tobacco.

"My name is Beaudelaire Talpas," said the rider, running his tongue around the inside of his mouth before spitting out a long trail of tobacco juice.

"And my name is Simms. You're late."

Talpas frowned and leaned back in his saddle, measuring Simms with unblinking, alert eyes. "Late? What the hell do you mean by that?"

"The fight is over. News came through but two weeks ago, saying the President himself had granted a pardon to those who had taken up arms."

"The Mormons?"

Simms nodded.

"Well, I ain't in the employ of no Mormons." The long-haired man's eyes twinkled with barely contained glee. "Not now."

"You're still late."

The humor slowly drained from his face. "And how is it you're knowing who I am?"

"People talk. I listen, see, remember."

"I see. Well," Talpas rolled his shoulders, lifted his backside from the saddle, farting loud and long. Grimacing, he settled back down in the saddle, which groaned under his weight. "That's what I think of President Buchanan and all those rascals over in Washington. Brigham Young, too. Never could quite grasp how they came to an agreement. Maybe Young will be given a Governorship." He jutted his chin towards the log cabin. "Mind if I ask you to tell the little lady to point her gun somewhere else?"

Without averting his stare, Simms nodded once. "Noreen, move back inside."

Wriggling like a snake, Noreen withdrew, soon swallowed up by the murkiness of the interior.

"She's still pointing it."

"As I told her to."

A change came over the face of the man on the horse, eyes narrowing, jaw clenched. "Now why would you do that?"

"I might ask you what you're doing here, coming onto my place?"

Talpas grunted, moved around in his saddle as if it were not quite to his liking, and sighed. "Just passing through."

"My advice would be to move on."

Talpas leaned over to his left and released a second trail of tobacco juice to the ground. "I don't much like being told what to do, mister."

"It's a suggestion."

"Simms, you said?" The detective nodded, unblinking. Talpas sneered. "Don't think I know what you do. For employment, I mean."

"No reason for you to."

Talpas mulled Simms's words over, chewing hard on his tobacco. "The way you wear your gun makes me think you know how to use it."

"I protect my own."

"Well, you have a mighty nice home here to protect. Let's hope it stays that way. Nice talking to you." Straightening himself up once more, Talpas flicked the reins, turned his horse about and slowly made his way back the way he had come.

The seconds trickled by, Simms remaining motionless until Noreen sidled beside him. Without a word, he slipped his arm around her waist. "Who was he," she said, voice barely above a whisper.

"Death on a horse, that's who he was."

Her face came up, her eyes big, full of fear. "You think he will come back?"

Simms gnawed at his bottom lip for a moment. "I reckon you could guarantee it."

Two

Pinkerton Central Office, Chicago, Illinois

Three months before Simms taught Noreen to shoot, he rolled into the main office of the Pinkerton Detective Agency in Chicago, Illinois. A stunned silence settled over the room, every face from every desk staring. Standing in the doorway, Simms met each of his colleagues' faces with icy resolve, wondering what their next reaction would be. He didn't have to wait long. The room erupted into a frenzy of wild cheering, backslapping and general merriment as colleagues rushed to him, congratulating him with unbridled delight. From somewhere, someone thrust a tumbler of whisky into his hand, whilst someone else broke out in song, but it all ceased as quickly as it had begun when the commander's office door swung open. An uneasy silence descended. Simms gave his excuses, edging his way through the press of beaming fellow detectives, and stood in front of Chesterton.

"I have to hand it to you, Simms, you did better than I expected."

This was as close to a compliment as Simms was going to get, and he smiled, tipping his hat. "General Russell was overcome with joy to be reunited with his daughter."

Chesterton grunted, then turned his gaze to the room where men were laughing and joking again, the tension easing. They drank too, perhaps more than Chesterton was prepared to allow. The big Commander of Detectives pulled in a breath and barked, "Get back to work. Party is over!"

Without a pause, the men obeyed the commands and scurried back to their desks, some muttering, most silent. Chesterton grunted again and waved Simms inside his office.

Simms pulled up short. A man sat with his back to him. Broad across the shoulders, he wore a brown tweed jacket, his lank, black hair falling to the collar. He swung around in his chair, face impassive, large, dark eyes studying the detective with a keen interest.

Simms felt a dryness in his throat, something he didn't normally experience when faced with another human being. But this man was different. He was his employer, Allan Pinkerton.

"Detective Simms," said Chesterton, moving around to the far side of his desk, "this is Mr. Allan Pinkerton, founder and director of our agency."

Simms nodded. "I recognize you from your photograph in the newspapers. Pleased to know you, sir." The detective stepped forward and shook the man's hand.

"Likewise." Pinkerton made no move to stand up but instead remained sitting, his eyes taking in the lean figure of Simms who, himself, offered no movement. He dropped his hand to his lap. "So, you read newspapers, Mr. Simms."

"When I get the chance."

"Yes, when you get the chance."

"Out on the range it's often difficult to keep abreast of news and the like."

Chesterton blew out a sigh and sat down, face dark with annoyance. Simms's gruff manner often had such an effect on the Chief of Detectives.

"You wear your guns like a gunfighter," remarked Pinkerton, motioning to the Colt Dragoon holstered at Simms's waist. Underneath his coat, another pistol rested in its holster under the detective's right armpit. "I'm not certain if such a display is warranted, certainly not here in Chicago. You could even be breaking the law by carrying such firearms, detective."

Simms tilted his head. "I have permits. As all detectives are so obliged. I'm no different."

"Even so."

Simms dragged his gaze from his employer to Chesterton, "Is this why I'm here? To be berated over carrying weapons?" Simms gave an easy smile. "After all I've done?"

Chesterton bristled, shot a glance towards Pinkerton, then back to his lead detective. "We have another situation, Simms."

"One that doesn't require me to shoot…" He turned again to Pinkerton. "Or kill?"

It was Pinkerton's turn to recoil a little. "Mr. Simms, what you accomplished out in the Territories was nothing short of a miracle. Not only with the rescue of Elisabeth Russell, but also your single-handed apprehension of those two heartless killers. You have promoted the work of our agency to dizzying heights. I was honored to be in the presence of the President only the other day, and listen to him commending us for the work we have done. So, I'm not criticizing you, Detective, I'm merely pointing out that perhaps, just perhaps, you should be a little more circumspect in your display of firearms. We have appearances to maintain now." He reached into his own coat and produced a small, black revolver.

But Simms was already moving. In a blur, the Colt Dragoon materialized in his right fist, pointing unerringly at Chesterton, with the other gun, a Navy Colt, levelled at Pinkerton. In the eerie stillness of the room, the heavy sound of the hammers cocking and cylinders being engaged, sent a chill through the air.

Chesterton managed a rattling, "Jesus, Simms."

"Don't ever pull a gun on me," said Simms through gritted teeth, his eyes glinting with a barely controlled menace towards Pinkerton. "If you do, you're a dead man, Mr. Pinkerton."

Pinkerton, frozen in the act of drawing the revolver, held up his other hand, palm outward. "Mr. Simms, I'm not about to shoot you."

"Doesn't seem that way from here."

"I beg you, please..."

"Simms, put the goddamned guns away," said Chesterton, the anger rumbling in his throat.

Simms blinked, but only once. "Lay it on the table, then step back."

"I have no intention of—"

"On the table, Mr. Pinkerton. Then you can explain why you pulled a gun on me."

Pinkerton nodded and with infinite care, settled the revolver on the tabletop. He looked up at Chesterton. "He's quite right, I should have warned him. My mistake." He turned to Simms. "You're a dangerous man to know, Mr. Simms. I'm not sure if I'm all that comfortable with such knowledge."

Simms holstered the Dragoon, but kept the Navy in his left fist. He stepped across to the table and lifted the smaller revolver Pinkerton had produced.

"It's a pocket-model Colt," explained Pinkerton. "My plan is to arm all of my detectives with this weapon, allowing them to maintain a modicum of decency whilst conducting their duties in the city. Its size allows for its positioning in a shoulder holster, not unlike your own, Detective, but without the overt display you seem so intent upon. Concealment and protection – that's my desire."

"You could have said."

"I do not need to explain myself to you, Detective. But, in this instance, you are correct. I should have pre-warned you." Pinkerton's smile returned. "Apologies."

Simms released his breath in a long stream. "Apology accepted." He slowly released the hammer of his Navy Colt and dropped it back into his holster, at the same time examining the pocket model more closely. "It's not even loaded."

"It is not my desire to walk around the great city of Chicago with a loaded gun, Detective. As I explained."

Simms looked up to catch Chesterton's enraged face. "You're awful close to crossing the line, Simms."

Pinkerton threw up his arms, "Ah, commander, the fault lies with me. Detective Simms is a man of the Frontier, a hardened, intrepid enforcer; a man who must react as instincts dictate. You fought in the Mexican War, so I understand?"

"Yes, I did."

"With some distinction, I've heard?"

"I wouldn't know about that."

"Really? You were mentioned in dispatches, on several occasions. I understand you refused a Certificate of Merit?"

"It wasn't something which much interested me – I never quite saw the reasons for honoring a man's ability to kill others."

"I believe you rescued a group of civilians who were being held in a church? You single-handedly—"

Holding up his hand, Simms cut off any further narration. "I don't care to talk about any of that, Mr. Pinkerton. It was all a very long time ago."

"Yes, but it made you into the resourceful and skillful individual you are now. Our agency has need of such talents."

"That's hardly the word I'd use for what I do."

"No, but nevertheless …" Shooting a quick glance towards Chesterton, Pinkerton sat back in his chair and sighed. "Very well, let's put this behind us and continue with what I came here to discuss." He smiled at Simms. "What I'm going to say will suit your particular attributes entirely, Detective Simms." He motioned Simms to another chair which stood in the far corner. "Please, sit down, and hear me out." He pointed to the pocket revolver. "You may keep that, for when you're next in Chicago."

"I already am."

"Yes. But not for much longer."

Simms sank into the nearby chair and listened to what this curious man had to say.

Three

Pulling open his cracked leather portmanteau, Simms slipped his two big revolvers inside. Sitting back in his chair, he examined the much smaller, pocket model Colt and moved the cylinder around, one notch at a time. With deliberate care, he raised it and took a bead along the short, stubby barrel. He grunted and looked across to where Henson was sifting through a pile of official-looking papers.

"The boss said you have the details," drawled Simms, already bored with the office, the paperwork, the fastidiousness of his colleagues. He dropped the revolver into his coat pocket. Being a hot day, he'd slung his coat across the back of his chair, and now ran his fingers underneath his collar, the perspiration building. "Damn, have you no air in this place?"

"I thought you'd be used to it, living out on the range."

"In the open is fine, in here, trussed up like a racoon in a cage, it's not."

"I've never seen a racoon in a cage."

"Then you have much to discover."

Henson frowned and dropped three sheets of paper in front of his colleague. "These are copies of the telegrams sent down the line after the first robbery."

"First robbery?" Interested now, Simms leaned forward and picked up the closest notification. He scanned the words, curling his tongue over his top lip as he often did when reading. When he'd read through all three, he leaned back in his chair and folded his arms. "All right, so give me the details."

"They hit the south bound train which had on board, amongst other things, the wages for the laborers working on the line extension. A pretty sum. One hundred and fifty thousand dollars."

Simms whistled. "Dear God Almighty."

"They have almost two thousand men working on this particular line, and that was their six-month retainer. As you can imagine, they ain't happy and production has stopped. The railroad company contacted the Government and that's where we come in."

"Wasn't it guarded?"

"The *train*?" Simms nodded and Henson sneered. "Of course it was. Four men, two in the railcar, which carried the money – stashed inside a two-inch solid steel safe. Another guard stood with the driver, one on the tailgate of the caboose. He was the first to die, shot from long range."

"Long range?"

"It was a hell of a thing. The gang laid several petrified tree trunks across the tracks, which slowed the locomotive, then they opened fire. There were five riders, according to the witnesses, so we're guessing there are at least six of them, given the sharp shooter must have been some distance away. After they'd shot the guard with the driver, they uncoupled the caboose and told the driver to pull away. With the caboose detached, they ordered the guards inside to open up. The brakeman apparently came out, hands above his head. A family man, name of Jeff Rivers. Worked for the company for ten years, one of the originals. When the guards refused to come out, they shot and killed Rivers without so much as a blink. The guards gave it up then."

"Sounds as if the gang were mighty determined."

"Murdering sons of bitches is what they are, Simms. Our agency doesn't operate in the West, not yet. But the President himself wants these men apprehended and brought to justice. He sees this sort of thing as a precursor to a whole lot more such incidents once the railroads move into the New Territories. What you did, bringing back the General's daughter, has impressed the railroad company no end."

"The Government too, so I'm led to believe."

"Seems that way. They've engaged us to help bring this situation to a conclusion." Henson lowered his voice, tone growing ominous. "But they want it done with extreme, brute force, to advertise to everyone that the government won't tolerate such crimes and will always pursue the perpetrators using the full weight of the law."

"Even if that means killing them?"

"If needs be. Those bastards killed something like seven people on that train, Simms. Once they blew open the safe, they set about relieving the few passengers of their personal possessions. One man stood up to them, retired army major by the name of Cartwright. He was travelling over to Laramie with his wife and son, a twenty-two-year-old, recently promoted to Second Lieutenant. When Cartwright stood up, the gang killed him stone dead, and tried to do the same with the son. The bullet hit him in the arm, a wound which may well end his soldering before it's even begun. The murderers left the widow to lament over the body of her—"

"All right, Henson," said Simms, holding up his hands in mock-surrender, "you've painted the picture well enough. These are dead men walking, is what you're saying."

"Is what I'm saying." Henson's index finger stabbed at the second paper. "Here are their physical descriptions, and further testimonies from witnesses. As far as we can ascertain, they made their way southwest. In one of the few remaining miners' towns, they shot up a saloon and got into a gunfight with a gang of roughnecks. One of the gang ended up dead. So that leaves five of them."

"Including the sharpshooter."

"Who took care of the roughnecks."

"How many were there?"

"Eight."

Simms held Henson's stare. "This sniper – for that's what he is – he killed all eight?"

Henson nodded. "His companions were holed up in the saloon, and the *sniper*, as you call him, *picked* off the attacking roughnecks, one by one."

Simms studied the descriptions of the gang, but as for the sharpshooter, there were no details.

"There's only one man I know who can shoot like that," said Simms. "His name is Samuel Brewer. I served with him back in the War. He's way too old now. Besides, this just isn't his style. But…" He picked up the papers, folded them and, swiveling around on his chair, stuffed them inside his jacket.

"But?"

"But, he might just know who else can shoot like that."

Henson grunted and placed a thick envelope on the desk. "Expenses. When you apprehend the robbers, process them at Fort Laramie. Telegraph us here, then we'll give you further instructions."

"Process? What sort of a word is that? You mean sling 'em over the back of a horse and claim the bounty?"

"You're not a bounty hunter, Simms. You're a Pinkerton Detective. For some reason, which I fail to understand, Chesterton is allowing you free-reign across the Territories, but you will be a paid a retainer, with bonuses when your assignment is completed. It's *not* a bounty. They're turning a blind eye to the bounty you took for Mason and Newhart." Henson slumped into his chair. "What are you going to do with that money anyways?"

"I've already done it. Bought a spread, built a little house. It was my intention to dabble in being a farmer, until I got the call from Mr. Pinkerton that is."

"You're not a farmer, Simms. You're a gunman. A shootist. A *pistolero*. Isn't that what they call people like you down Mexico way?"

"People like me? Jesus, Henson, if you're not careful, your halo's gonna slip."

"What the hell do you mean by that?"

"I mean," and he stood up, tugging on his jacket, "you're a self-righteous bastard who needs to get his fat ass out of this office and into a saddle. Until you've ridden the range, Henson, you've got no right to judge."

"You shouldn't be a Pinkerton, Simms. You're too damned wild."

"And if I wasn't, Henson, who would go after men like those bastards?" He cocked a single eyebrow. "*You?*" He shook his head, picked up the portmanteau and tipped his hat. "I'll see you in a few weeks, Henson. Until then, don't get your hands too dirty. You may need to type out another telegram."

He swung away and left the office without a further glance, knowing Henson would sit and seethe with no words to counter what Simms had said.

Four

A Reunion in Chicago

Meeting with old man Brewer was akin to visiting the past. The former sergeant major greeted Simms like a long-lost son, bear-hugging him on the porch of his house in downtown Chicago.

"My God in heaven, it's good to see you," said Brewer, studying the lean detective with affection. "You're looking so fit and healthy."

Simms smiled, somewhat self-consciously, and had to use considerable force to pry himself free of the man's grip. "You too, Sam," Simms lied, for the old man's features were drawn, etched with melancholy and perhaps something more. "Are you keeping well?"

"Aches and pains, more each day, but what the hell? I'm seventy-four, so I can't complain." He stepped aside and waved Simms into the narrow hallway.

The house smelled of lavender and primrose, not at all what Simms was expecting from a man he'd shared whole months out on the plains with, living in slits in the ground, exposed to the elements, bathed in their own, stinking sweat. Brewer must have noticed his former companion's expression and he grinned. "That's Alison, God bless her."

"Alison? Your wife?"

"No, no. My daughter. She comes to call every day, cooks me dinner, cleans and tidies the house. She insists on washing everything down with lavender water. Not sure where I'd be without her." He led Simms down the hall into a small, freshly painted room with French doors looking out onto a tiny patch of grass surrounded by flowerbeds. A round table, covered with a white linen embroidered cloth, nestled next to the window, with two chairs pushed underneath. A single armchair sat in front of the empty fireplace. In wintertime, the room would be snug and warm, but right now, with summer at its height, the heat radiated from the walls, making the atmosphere close and uncomfortable. Brewer, reacting to his guest's changed mood, immediately crossed to the windows and pushed them open.

"I must admit, I tend to feel the cold far more than I used to," said Brewer, "but the weather is mighty hot right now."

Simms smiled his thanks. "Not like when we were out on the prairie, struggling to survive."

"I never knew cold like it, until now. My old bones are as thin as cotton yarn. Things change."

"That they do. Are you sure you're all right, Sam? You seem a tad peaky."

Shrugging, Brewer crossed over to the door. "I'll make some coffee," he said and went out, leaving Simms to scan the room.

Above the fireplace, standing on the mantle, a small painting in a gilded frame peered out at him. Bending close, he regarded the image of a young woman. Exquisitely rendered in oils, it appeared as lifelike as any of the new-fangled photographs he'd first seen in Harper's Weekly, a journal which appeared only the year before. He supposed the painting was of Alison, Brewer's daughter and thought no more of it as he turned to look around.

Sparsely decorated, apart from the few pieces of furniture, the room presented an austere aspect, with very little in the way of possessions to lend it any sense of warmth. Lonely. Despite the heat, Simms shivered and stepped across to the only other object, a single painting hanging at a skewed angle on the wall opposite the window. Studying it, he took in the backdrop of soaring, snow-topped mountains, in the foreground a lone Indian warrior gazing out across the crystal-clear water of a vast lake. Swallowed up by the image, he imagined himself out there, surrounded by the vastness of the wild, untamed land. The lure of the open range, the windswept prairie, the solitude; this was where he felt more alive than anywhere else. Back in forty-seven, when he sprawled down in the dirt to fight his first battle against the Mexicans, he'd learned to love the land. Its bleak, unremitting harshness set a fire alight inside his soul. Town life wasn't for him. Even when he went across to Illinois and took up the position with the Pinkertons less than half a dozen years after the War ended, it was never his intention to live in the city, any city for that matter.

Preferring the endless, breathtaking beauty of the plains, that was where his true home lay. And this painting mirrored every emotion such places brought to him.

"Beautiful, isn't it."

Brewer had come up to him unnoticed and Simms smiled as he took the proffered coffee in both hands. He sipped it and nodded with satisfaction. "That's good." Turning to the painting again, he gave a long sigh. "*This* is more than good, Sam. Where did you get it?"

"I painted it."

Simms snapped his head around, surprised beyond words. "*You?* Dear God, I never knew you could do anything like this."

"I've always painted. Even when we were in that filthy war, I would often spend my time sketching. I'll show you, if you like."

They settled down around the table and Brewer produced a dog-eared sketchbook. As he thumbed the pages, Simms gazed in silent awe at the drawings. Drawings of soldiers, horses, Mexican prisoners sitting cross-legged, eating from wooden bowls, guards watching over them. Shoshone warriors astride ragged ponies, mountain ranges and winding rivers. There must have been thirty or more such scenes.

"I had no idea," said Simms, his voice barely above a whisper.

"I gave up after Elizabeth passed away." He motioned towards the painting above the fireplace. "Alison took some other portraits I did of her, but that one…" He fell silent for a moment, staring into something far away.

"I'm sorry," said Simms, uneasy, not knowing how to respond with any great sense of understanding. Marriage, loved and being loved, these were alien concepts to him. He recognized people's pain at losing someone close, but how to react with meaning he simply did not know.

"She was taken by scarlet fever three years ago this fall. There's never a day goes by when I don't think of her."

"She's very beautiful."

"Yes. She was." He sniffed, pulling himself out of his reverie and turned his gaze upon the detective. "Drink your coffee, then tell me what brings you here."

Returning to study the exquisite drawings, Simms took his time to gather his thoughts. He drank his coffee then, when nothing remained but the dregs in the bottom of his cup, he leaned back in his chair. "There's been an incident, out West." Simms ran his tongue over his lips, savoring the last remnants of his drink. "Seems like a team of desperadoes attacked a train, killing the guards and some passengers. The Pinkertons have assigned me to apprehend them, bring them to justice."

"I'd heard you were now a detective."

Simms arched an eyebrow, but let the obvious question of how Brewer had come by such news sit inside. "One of the guards was shot, from a distance. Crack shot. Expertly done."

"So, you thought you'd come and ask me if I have an inkling."

"You were the finest sharpshooter in the whole government army back in forty-seven. You trained the best."

"I retired not long after that, already too old to be carrying out my duties."

"But you trained men."

"I trained you."

"Yes, you did. And mighty well, may I say." Brewer nodded once, in appreciation of Simms's praise. "Who else?"

"I trained a lot. Some of them went on to become drill sergeants themselves. It might be more profitable to interview them." Brewer shrugged. "I'm not being deliberately obtuse, but I've lost touch with all of that. The man to ask is a certain Josiah Edwardson. He went out and joined the Texas Rangers not long after the War. He was the finest marksman I ever knew. He'd be the man I'd go see."

"Out Texas?" Simms chuckled, "I haven't got the time. And Texas..." He shook his head. "No one from Texas is going to travel up to Colorado to hold up a train. I doubt anyone in Texas knows what a train is."

"You could be right." Brewer flicked through the pages of his sketchbook, thinking hard. "I hear the Territories are wild, unchartered, not the sort of place to settle down in. Indians – Utes, Bannocks, Shoshone. An unforgiving place."

"A lot of mean white folk too, Sam. Some meaner than any native, believe you me."

"You were there. I followed the story."

Simms shifted uncomfortably in his chair. "I didn't know it was reported."

"Oh yes. The newspapers here, they have a keen interest in anything that goes on in the West. You brought in old Russell's daughter, so the story goes. Kidnapped, wasn't she?"

"She was, although what the men who took her were hoping to achieve is difficult to fathom. All those varmints succeeded in was burning a trail of death and destruction through every town and homestead they came upon."

"But you killed them?"

"That I did." Simms released a long breath. "In the end."

"And now, you're on the hunt again."

"This sharpshooter, he's stone cold, Sam. There's no telling who he might kill next."

"I recall there was a man. He wasn't as good as Edwardson; had neither the endless patience nor the single-mindedness that dear old Josiah possessed. But he was cruel, enjoyed what he did, relished the explosion of the melons we set out on the fence rails five hundred yards from where the shooters took aim. Very few could hit those targets with the precision of that man, but I always felt he did it, not with a professional's eye, but with that of a sadistic killer." Brewer shook his head. "He longed for those exploding fruits to be human heads. I could sense it."

"What was his name?"

"Ishmael Farage. Last I heard, he'd gone West to kill Indians for the mining companies out Colorado way. Now that most of those places are almost spent, he could well have fallen in with those following less *honourable* professions, such as the ones you describe. I reckon such work would suit him. A calling, you might say." Brewer levelled Simms with a hard stare. "A calling for killing."

For a long time, the silence hung in the air. At last, after several moments, Simms stretched out his legs. "Well, Sam. I think you might have given me something, for which I'm grateful. I shall be setting out early tomorrow, but until then…" He smiled. "I seem to recall you were always a connoisseur of good Irish whiskey." Simms cocked his head. "Or has your beloved Alison put paid to that particular avenue of pleasure?"

Brewer's own smile spread across his face. "No, she has not. And I'm impressed with your memory." He slapped his knees and stood up. "Only thing is, I'm not sure if I have any glasses. Would your coffee cup do?"

"If you have Irish whiskey, Sam, I'll drink it out of my shoe."

They both laughed, but when Sam went out to fetch the bottle, Simms fell into a dark, depressed mood, for now he knew who his quarry was, and of what such a man was capable.

Five

The unchartered territories of the West

Simms repeated the exact same journey he'd first made when circumstances had forced him west, less than a year before. There were some differences – new homesteads, a cluster of buildings heralding the birth of a new town – but the land itself remained the same. Arid, harsh; the heat unrelenting. At the rail terminus, he alighted and secured himself a horse, together with supplies and enough water to get him across the prairie to Fort Bridger.

The Fort, now rebuilt, bristled with troops when Simms walked his horse towards the Army livery stables. The war against the Mormons had flickered out to nothing more than a few smoldering hotspots. Up until now no one had died, a fact which brought a sense of relief to Simms as he waited for Colonel Johnstone to return to his command tent. A war without death was a rare thing indeed, but perhaps the only welcome kind.

The Colonel, when he blustered through the canvas flaps, looked as he always did. Aloof, angry, jowls red with either stress or something else. Simms doubted it was drink. Johnstone was a hard, unforgiving man, but one who took his responsibilities seriously.

Studying the detective with narrowed eyes, Johnstone stood with hands on hips, jaw jutting forward. "I heard you were back, news which I must admit filled me with foreboding. What is it this time, another kidnapping?"

"Robberies. The railroad companies are growing jittery. I'm here to bring a bunch of bandidos who robbed a train to justice. Thought I'd pay my respects on the way."

"That's civil of you, Detective." Johnstone pulled off his dirt-caked duster and threw it into the corner. "I've just come from a meeting with a bevy of commanders of the Nauvoo Legion." He clenched his teeth, "Man, they are not an easy bunch to bargain with. But with Brigham Young and the President cozying up together, it seems this spot of trouble is over before it even began. We're not taking anything for granted, mind you. Calhoon is camped up at the Colorado River Ferry with a troop, so not much has changed."

"The train-robbers, they went south west, so I understand. They shot up a mining town then moved out. That's my first port of call. A place called Brentville, whatever that means."

"Tobias Brent. Made a small fortune mining gold before the seam ran out. I knew him. A weasel of a man, shifty, not afraid to bend a few arms to get his own way, if you understand my meaning."

"He has his own mining company?"

"He did. Got himself killed in a poker game about six months back. Left everything to his wife and partner, who later got himself elected as sheriff. I don't know much about him, but he may know something about your quarry, as they shot up the town fairly badly."

"So you heard about it?"

Grunting, Johnstone moved behind his desk and pulled out the top drawer. He rummaged around inside and brought out a bottle of whiskey and two small tumblers, which he filled. He thrust out his hand and Simms took the drink. They both raised their arms before throwing down their respective drinks. Simms nodded in appreciation.

"News of what happens right across the territories tends to filter over to here eventually. I had no idea that what happened over in Brentville was linked to the train robberies, but you're saying it's the same gang?"

"So I understand. This bunch, they have a sharpshooter riding with them. He's good. Damned good."

"I know." Simms frowned and Johnstone explained. "I spoke with Major Cartwright's boy. Damned shame what happened to him."

"He told you the details?"

"Every last one. Said he heard the gunshot, which took out the guard at the back of the train, then saw the other robbers coming through the carriage. They didn't wear any disguises. Guess that gives you some idea of just how arrogant and dangerous these men are. Looks like they weren't planning on leaving many witnesses; traumatizing any who saw them by killing some others. You know what it's like yourself, in such stressful situations – you don't notice much."

"But he did."

"Young Cartwright? Yes, he did, enough to give the Marshalls' office a good description. An artist made sketches, and distributed them on posters. The usual thing."

"But not one of the sharpshooter."

"No. Cartwright never saw him. Must be one helluva shot though, whoever he is."

"So, where is the boy now?"

"He's stayed here, Detective."

"Here?"

"Yes, that's right." Johnstone leaned forward. "When he heard about you, he decided to stick around and meet you. I have a notion he wants to help."

"Well, he's in for a disappointment – I work alone."

"Thing is, I'm thinking the boy ain't gonna take 'no' for an answer. He's been taking lessons, learning how to shoot left-handed. He's intent on revenge, Detective."

"Seems to me, with only one usable arm, he's not going to be much good, is he? More of a burden if anything. How's he gonna reload his gun?" Simms massaged his forehead. "I'm not a nurse-maid, God damn it."

"He's not an invalid! He can't make a fist is all. The bullet hit his forearm, mashed up his ligaments and such. He looks the same as you and me, saving he can't hold anything of any weight in his right hand. But he can shoot, and he's got sand, by God. If you turn him down, he'll go after them anyway."

"And get himself killed."

"Well, you'd better do what you can to prevent it. If conscience dictates, of course. If not, you can rest easy knowing you'd be responsible for his death and even further trauma for his poor, ailing mother."

Simms, with his mouth half-open, stared at Johnstone in disbelief. "You really know how to ladle it on, don't you?"

Johnstone shrugged. "For pity's sake, Simms, just take the poor kid along. He wants to help, *do* something, try to wipe away the memory of seeing his father die in such a way. Wouldn't you want to do the same?"

Johnstone's voice sounded tired. He looked tired too; deep, black shadows ringed his eyes, lines of worry etched across his forehead. Simms felt the resistance seep away as he thought over the Colonel's words, knowing his own determination to avenge an act so cowardly and unwarranted would win through. Exhaling slowly, he allowed his shoulders to drop, accepting the inevitable. "Very well. Where do I find him?"

"I sent a message to Laramie. He'll be here in the morning."

"Seems like you had all this arranged even before I agreed."

Johnstone smiled. "You're a man of honor, Detective. I know that much."

"And if I'd refused?"

The Colonel's smile broadened into a full grin. "Well, who knows? Perhaps you'd be delayed a little, get into a fight, be arrested and thrown into the brig?" Johnstone sucked his teeth, shaking his head as if highly amused by the whole situation. "Simple truth is, I knew the boy's father. We'd served together, and I'd like to see the bastards who murdered Cartwright put in the ground. The boy seems hell bent on doing just that and I for one, have no concerns over the method. You help him, Detective. In whatever way you have to. I want those bastards pegged out in the midday sun, their eyelids sewn back. I want them to suffer; you understand what I'm saying?"

"I hear you, Colonel. But are you sure this boy is up to it?"

"I know he is. But, just in case, I've harnessed you with an Indian tracker by the name of Deep Water. He's as fine a tracker as you'll find in these parts, and he hates every God-fearing white man from here to the Pesos. He'll point you in the right direction, mark my words."

"So, an Indian *and* a one-armed army recruit. You sure know how to make me feel real comfortable about this situation, Colonel."

"I knew you'd see it my way, Detective."

"It ain't *my* way, Colonel, I can assure you of that."

"You just find those sonsofbitches. That's all you need worry about. You got it?"

"I got it."

"Good. Now get out of my goddamned tent and be on your way. I have an entire territory to look after."

Simms screwed up his mouth, put the glass on top of the Colonel's desk, turned and went outside. He took in a large lungful of air and gazed towards the sky. He hoped, in that single moment, it wouldn't be long until he was back home, in his newly-created log cabin farm, with the woman who had given him a silver lining to look forward to. Noreen. He smiled at the thought of her, and tramped across the sprawling camp toward the livery stable, his horse, and the next stage of this unwanted endeavor.

Six

The open range, two day's ride from Fort Bridger

The man stood on the buckboard of his covered wagon, hands held aloft, railing against the sky. "My God, can you hear me? Heavenly Jesus, the truth is with you. Bring it to us all, I beseech you!"

His wild eyes settled on the cluster of bedraggled Navaho, drawn to this strange individual by his screeching voice and brightly colored clothes. The warriors had left camp on a hunting party two days ago, leaving old men, women, and children to scratch around in the dirt. When the stranger came amongst them, he offered the old men whisky. None refused – they liked whisky. Firewater they called it and they drank fitfully, dancing around, voices raised in glee. The women, huddling together some distance away, turned down their mouths, exchanging troubled stares. Something wasn't right.

"I am here to bring you the word of God," the stranger continued, brandishing a dog-eared, well-thumbed book. His jacket and trousers were of fawn-colored fabric, with patches of blue and yellow stitched with red and green thread. His entire garb, an erratic mix, went well with his shock of white hair, and the straggling, unkempt beard.

One old man, wizened, his naked torso baked almost black by the sun, waggled a finger towards the stranger. "What is this truth?"

"My friend," cried the stranger, settling his gaze upon the old man, "seek not to question the ways of God, but to accept His divine majesty!"

"You speak in riddles," spat the old man and turned away, taking a mouthful of whisky from the bottle handed to him by the stranger not minutes before.

"We cannot hope to understand the ways of our Lord," continued the stranger. "I bring you hope, salvation, and freedom from the toil which is your life."

He dipped inside the wagon and returned with a handful of books, not unlike his own, which he threw to various people mingling around the wagon. "The word of the Lord," he said.

A woman caught one of the books, opened it and frowned. "This is white man's writing. I have seen this before. We cannot understand this." She threw it back and the book hit the stranger in the midriff before falling to the ground. The stranger watched it spill to the dirt, his expression growing dark. "You are a mad man," the woman shouted. "You wait for our husbands and brothers to leave camp, and you come here with these mad words. Why do you come here?"

From nowhere, an arrow thudded into the side panel of the wagon, inches away from where the stranger stood.

They stopped, the clamor dying. Everyone waited.

The stranger's face came up, brewing with a new kind of malevolence. "Who did that? Would you try to kill me, a messenger from God?"

"What is it you want?"

They all turned and looked. A low murmuring rumbled from the small crowd and the women and old men shuffled to the side, children gripped by the neck, yanked backwards.

A man moved forward. Once, his strength was impressive. Now, the flesh sagged from his still-thick arms. His torso carried the shadows of hard muscle, the belly shrunken, the chest slack. Despite his stooped shoulders, he stood a good head above everyone else, his authority glowering from every pore, every knotted sinew. In his gnarled hands was the bow he'd used to fire the arrow.

"I come to bring you salvation – the mercy of the Lord," said the stranger.

"Mercy? I do not know this word."

"Then you should, for it is the greatest of all words. By following the Lord, you will achieve His forgiveness, for you are lost."

The big Indian tilted his head. "More riddles. I ask you again, white man. What is it you want?"

The stranger held the Indian's gaze, unblinking. After a prolonged pause, he let out a deep sigh, shoulders sagging. "I want *him*."

He brought up his arm, the index finger pointing directly behind the tall Indian. Everyone turned and looked towards where another white man sat, bound to an old, rotten stump of a tree. His uncovered head lolled on his chest and dried blood trailed from his mouth to the sweat-drenched front of his vest.

"He is an animal," said the tall Indian, fixing his stare towards this other man.

"Yes. But I want him."

More murmurings from the crowd, louder this time. A ripple of fear ran through them and the tall Indian nocked a second arrow. "Tell us, man of strange words, why you want this animal?"

Without a pause, the stranger jumped down from the buckboard, grunting as he hit the ground. "I need to speak with him, and I will exchange more whisky and the Lord's good book for just a few moments with him."

"Your books are worthless."

The stranger came up alongside the tall Indian. They were almost the same height, and as their eyes met, the stranger smiled. "But the whisky is good, yes?"

"We will take your whisky anyway."

The stranger's smile turned into a sneer and something flickered in the tall Indian's face; something that no one had seen before.

Fear.

In a blur, the stranger reached inside his coat and whipped out a revolver, pressing it into the tall Indian's guts, and fired.

The blast resounded impossibly loud, echoing across the wide, open prairie and a single, piercing scream issued from the tall Indian before he fell like lead to the ground.

Pandemonium erupted. The tiny crowd broke and fled in all directions, women scooping up their children in terror as through them strode the stranger, the gun smoking in his hand, no longer the conveyor of strange, unfathomable words but single-minded now, indifferent to the mayhem around him.

The second white man lashed to the stump brought up his head on the stranger's approach, took in a rattling breath and drawled through his cracked and broken mouth, "Hello Ned."

Ned stooped down and aimed his revolver at the man's forehead. "You sure is a difficult man to find, Harris. I been looking for you all over this goddamned territory."

"So now you found me." Harris coughed, straining at the cords binding him. "Set me free, would you?"

Ned twisted his mouth. "Not sure about that. Why they truss you up this way, them Indians?"

"I took one of their women," Harris sneered. "Them bucks, they caught up with me out in the mountains, beat me to shit and dragged me back here. Then they went off a-hunting. Told me that when they came back, they'd split my balls and peg me out to bake in the sun."

"And the squaw?"

"She fought like a wild-cat. I may have hit her somewhat hard."

"You mean you killed her?" Harris nodded, his eyes dropping, exhaustion etched into every cut and bruise of his broken face. His body convulsed into a sudden bout of painful sounding coughing. Ned waited until Harris ceased. "You always have had a knack of doing the wrong thing, especially where women is concerned."

"Set me free, Ned," Harris wailed, throwing back his head. "My wrists are cut through to the bone."

"Where is it?" Ned pushed the gun's muzzle into the man's forehead. "Where have you put the money?"

"Go to hell."

Ned eased back the hammer. "I'll kill you."

"Then you'll never find it."

Ned considered the truth of these words and was about to speak when a shadow fell over him. He spun on his heels, fanning the hammer, putting two shots into an old warrior's body. The man staggered backwards, gasping, crumpled to the ground, and died, the tomahawk slipping from his lifeless fingers. Beyond him, amongst the debris of the camp, the remaining people were running, gathering up their belongings, dragging along wailing children, and making good their escape. Ned turned again to Harris. "I just want what is mine, is all. I've been searching for these last ten days, since we all split up after Brentville. My patience has run thin, so just tell me where the fuck you put the goddamned gold."

"I ain't put it anywhere. Lol and the boys have it."

"That's not what we agreed, and you know it. We were meant to meet up at the hideout, split the money, then go our separate ways. I sat there like some sniveling idiot, waiting, waiting, waiting. You sucker-punched me and now I want what's due."

Harris licked his cracked lips before his head lolled to his chest. Ned gripped him by the chin, forcing his face upwards. Harris moaned, the whining tone of his voice reaching a new level. "Lol – he's got it, not me. I swear to God, Ned. He did the same with me, I swear. In the panic, we just got split up, is all. I'm sure Lol will do good by us all. He ain't no double-crosser."

"And where is he, eh? Where did he go?"

"Damned if I know. Cut me loose, Ned, and we'll go and search for him together. But please, cut me loose. Those heathen bastards beat me up good. I need a drink and these ropes is hurtin' bad."

"Where is Lol?"

"Jesus, don't you listen? *I don't know.*"

"Then take a guess. Your best guess. He must have had an alternative place to go. Lol was always good at planning things out. Tell me, then I'll cut you loose, give you water, and we'll ride out together, take a wide berth, well away from these heathen savages."

"I don't believe you."

"You ain't got no choice."

Harris chewed at his bottom lip. "Okay. Cut me loose, Ned. I'll ride with you and I'll show you the way."

"So you do know."

"Maybe I do. An idea anyway. If you kill me, you'll have no chance of finding anything. Cut me loose."

"You're full of shit."

Harris tried to smile, but only managed a twisted snarl. "And you, Ned, are in it, right up to your neck. Once the hunting party returns, they'll come after you, after what you've done here today. In that big old wagon of yours, you'll not get far. Cut me loose and I can help you. Two guns is better than one."

Ned nodded, accepting the truth and sense of his former companion's wise words. He reached behind him for the dead Indian's hatchet and hefted it in his hand. A movement caught his eye and he looked up to see a young boy, perhaps twelve years old, with a bow and arrow in his hands. The boy stood, his face a perfect mask of hatred as he slowly drew back the bowstring. Ned groaned. "Why don't things ever go my way, Lord," he asked aloud and the boy released his arrow.

Seven

The Indian camp

Harris squealed, averting his head when the young boy's head erupted in a mangled blast of shredded brain and bone. His wrecked body collapsed onto the ground. But his arrow, released in the moment the bullet from the unseen marksman hit home, thudded into Ned's shoulder, pitching him backwards. Writhing in the dirt, he kicked out his legs as the pain burned through his limb.

"Oh, God Almighty!" screamed Ned, rolling over, gripping the shaft of the arrow. "God Almighty, I'm a dead man for sure."

Amidst the mayhem of the camp, with some people running, others crouching behind whatever shelter available, and all wailing, a woman stumbled towards the remains of the dead child. She fell to her knees, hands and head aloft, beseeching invisible spirits to make amends. But no one, gods or otherwise, could undo the horror of that terrible moment. The woman took what remained of the child in her arms and rocked him backwards and forwards, sobbing with such heart-wrenching grief that Harris himself was brought to tears. He cared nothing for Ned and his wound, thoughts centering on the poor woman, clearly the child's mother, and the immensity of her loss. He tore his eyes from her and looked out across the plain.

A rider, tall in the saddle, approached; aloof, arrogant.

Harris sniffed hard, wishing his hands were free to wipe away the tears, which stung his eyes and ran like tiny rivulets through the grime of his face. Nevertheless, he managed to focus on the figure on the horse. A big man, long haired, riding with slow determination. Harris knew him and the dread welled up from within, overcoming everything else.

Any remaining natives scattered, making for the nearby, rock-strewn hillsides, for a demon had come into their world and fear overcame them, severing even the oppressive heat. This sense of dread settled over the surroundings like thick, threatening storm clouds and Harris watched, mesmerized as the stranger reigned in his horse to study the wailing woman next to the dead child. "The lamentations of the lost," he said, before considering the squirming Ned and finally Harris. "Howdy."

Over to the left, Ned, now on his knees, his face stretched taut with pain, had his eyes closed as he tugged at the offending dart in his shoulder. "I'm dying, goddamnit."

"You ain't dead yet," said the man on the horse. He drew out one of the twin Navy Colt's at his waist, and shot Ned through the head. The echo of the blast reverberated through the now almost deserted camp as Ned's body keeled over, sending up a small cloud of dust as it settled on the dry, broken ground. Rolling something around inside his mouth, the man leaned forward and spat out a long trail of brown tobacco juice towards the corpse. His aim was as near perfect as his gun shot, and a splat of dark brown spittle spread out across Ned's chest. "You is now," he said and he blew down the smoking barrel and grinned towards Harris. "You got the money?"

"Oh, dear Christ," whispered Harris, trying in vain to push himself farther away from this monster of a man. But the tree stump blocked his retreat and he put back his head and cried, "This ain't happening. I don't deserve none of this."

"Sure you do," said the stranger. He dropped the Navy Colt back into its holster and eased himself down from his saddle. The horse scraped at the ground but made no further movement, the merest flickering of its ears the single reaction it made to the gunshot.

Next to the stranger, the mother, oblivious to anything else, moaned and continued with her rocking, pressing her face into the body of the boy, grief total. But as the stranger's shadow fell over her, she jumped to her feet, a sudden determined wildness gripping her, and in her fist a knife, its blade chipped; rusty, yet dangerous. She flew forward, but the stranger turned, his body crouched, the gun appearing in his hand as if out of thin air, and he shot her in the chest.

Again, the horse made no movement.

And again, another body dropped to the ground, dead.

"Damned if there ain't no one left to kill," said the stranger, holstering the Navy again. He raised a single eyebrow as he glanced over to Harris. "Unless you want to join them, that is."

"Oh God. Oh God."

"Quit your squawking, you stinking fool. Tell me where the hell the money is."

Eyes growing wider, Harris stared at the stranger. "You him, ain't you?" He swallowed hard, throat constricted, dry with terror and thirst. "The one Lol told us about."

"Where is our good friend, Lol? Seems like he came up mighty short when he didn't show at our arranged meeting place." He nodded across to what remained of Ned. "Saw him waiting, mooching around like a whore with no customers. Followed him, figuring he'd lead me to where the money is. Seems like I was wrong in that assumption."

"I think I know where Lol is."

"Then you'd best tell me. I am not a man to be trifled with."

"I know it, believe you me." Harris nodded frantically. "Can you spare me some water?"

Blowing out his cheeks, the stranger went to his horse and unhooked a leather canteen from the saddle, pulled out the cork stopper and crossed over to Harris. "Open your mouth." Harris did so. The stranger tipped the canteen and a trail of water poured into Harris's waiting mouth, forcing him to splutter and cough. Despite this, he grinned his thanks, gasping loudly.

"Now," said the stranger, returning the canteen to his saddle. "Tell me."

"Cut me loose. These cords. My wrists are cut through to the bone."

"I'll cut you loose, then we get the hell out of here." He looked across to the distant horizon. "I have a feeling the bucks will be here before long, and my feelings are usually accurate. What the hell is that wagon yonder?"

Harris shrugged as his eyes followed to where the stranger gestured. Ned's bizarre-looking carriage stood waiting, the old, sinewy nag that pulled it hanging its head, gazing at the arid ground. "I reckon Ned picked it up from some travelling apothecary. Ned had no clue about medicines and such. Perhaps he was using it as a disguise."

The stranger grunted. "He must have come across it not so long ago. I've been tracking him for almost two days, never laid eyes on no travelling medicine-man."

"Well, it ain't Ned's, I know that much."

Another grunt. "You unhitch the horse and you can ride it. Bareback. You might find a blanket around here somewhere, but we have to be might quick, boy. Once them bucks return and find what has happened here, they will be on our trail quicker than a rattler after a rat." He grinned and winked at Harris. "Not that I'm no rat, you understand, but I'm no friend of any rattler and those bucks is pure poison, believe you me." Reaching behind his back, he tugged out a heavy-bladed Bowie knife, ran a finger along the blade and mumbled something in satisfaction. "You make a run for it, boy, and I'll kill you – money or no money. We have an understanding?"

"We sure do, mister, sir. "

The stranger cut Harris free and together, they left the camp on their respective mounts, leaving behind them the scene of carnage without a second's thought.

In the still of that evening, some hours after the two white men had left, the hunting party returned and sat stock-still, stunned at what they saw.

"Little Spring's defiler has left," said one of them, pointing to the tree stump where they had tied Harris the day before.

"You think the defiler did all of this, Tall Mountain?"

A well-built, heavily muscled warrior, head and shoulders above the others, eased his pony forward, and scanned the open ground. Turning his gaze to the east, his voice trembled with anger. "Two horses. Two men. Someone came to help the defiler."

"And killed another pale face before leaving," said a fourth warrior, on his haunches, studying the remains of Ned, the squaw, and her son. "They will suffer for this."

"I will take out their entrails," said Tall Mountain, his voice flat, his anger overcome, "and cook them in the sun whilst they lie and watch."

"We follow them now?"

Tall Mountain nodded. He motioned to three other warriors. "We cannot delay, so we go now and ride them down. The rest of you gather our people and break up camp. We cannot stay in this place, not after what has happened here. Leave the white bastard to rot, but take our own to the burial ground." He ground his teeth. "We will overtake the two pale bastards in a few days and make them weep for what they have done here today."

The others whooped and roared, brandishing their weapons. With a flick of his heels, Tall Mountain turned his horse, gesturing for the three chosen warriors to follow him. Together, they filed out of the camp and headed east, following the trail of the two white men so clearly written in the soil.

Eight

On the trail moving west

On the morning of the second day, with the sun a blinding, burning orb dominating the sky, they camped by a small stream. Under the shade of large, overhanging rocks, Deep Water cooked a buck-rabbit he had caught earlier, turning it on a makeshift spit until the flesh fell from its bones, the fat sizzling in the flames.

The men ate in silence and afterwards, Simms went down to the river, scooping up handfuls of water to throw over his face. He scanned the far bank, the uniform, sand-colored ground broken with the occasional patch of gorse; hardy plants struggling to survive in such a harsh, unforgiving environment. "I fought in places like this," he said as if to himself. "I hated it then, and I hate it still." Sighing, he stood and wandered back to the camp.

Forrest Cartwright lay down with a contented sigh, dipping his hat over his eyes. Within seconds he was fast asleep, his snore a deep, rumbling gurgle. Simms sat a few paces away, cleaning out the cylinders of his revolver, preparing two new ones with powder and ball, sealing them with wax. The scout watched him from afar, his eyes unblinking, interest gripped by the detective and his careful preparations.

"I have never liked guns," he said, as if making an aside.

Simms, not looking from his work, shrugged. "I might say the same about a bow and arrow. Each to his own, I guess."

"They are dirty things," continued Deep Water. "With the bow, it is silent, clean. And the arrow can be reused if the shaft is unbroken. The rabbit, he never knew I was there."

"Well," said Simms, dusting off his hands on his trousers, "they are dirty, I'll grant you that. I heard there is a new type, with what they call cartridges, which are like a tiny tube, with powder and ball already sealed inside. Makes reloading a whole lot faster, that's for sure. I wish I had a bunch of them right now." He raised his revolver, closed one eye, and studied it closely. "The thing about weapons, is human beings will always find a better way to kill someone. I reckon one day, someone will invent a weapon that can kill an entire town – hell, maybe even a city." He gave the gun a final wipe with an oily cloth and slipped it back into its holster. "People and killing are bosom buddies. It's just the way it is."

"My people have used the bow since the beginning of time," said Deep Water, considering the rabbit leg in his hand. He took a piece between his teeth and munched it down. "I see no need to change."

"Some of your people do not think the same. In raids against the whites, Indians have used guns. My fear is bad-minded men will sell more guns to your people, make them more dangerous. Perhaps, in a few years, this will lead to war."

"And we will kill one another using those same weapons."

"Yes. But we'll blame you, not ourselves. We take your land and when you protest, we kill you. And when you kill us, our hatred knows no bounds. The problem is, of course, we forget that we too came from somewhere. We think of this land as ours, that we have some sort of God-given right to do with it as we please."

"The Great Spirit, this god you talk about, he gave this land to everything which breathes." He held up the remains of the rabbit leg. "He gives us food, but if we are greedy and take it all, what then? We starve. It is the same with land. You white people, you want it all."

"Your people, you will resist so there will be war."

"A war none of us can win. White people are more plentiful than the grass. I think maybe this land will belong to only them one day and when that day comes…" His expression grew darker still. "When you have taken everything, you will perish, fighting amongst yourselves for whatever remains. You are a destructive people and you do not care what you destroy to take whatever it is you want."

Deep Water lapsed into silence, his eyes glazing over as if he were sinking within himself. Perhaps, Simms mused, that was why he was so named. Coming across Indians was not a common practice for the Pinkerton, but those whom he confronted were of the more brutal variety. Deep Water, sanguine, slow and deliberate, seemed to be closer to what Simms had always considered the nobler aspects of the Native. Watching the way he conducted himself, Simms knew here was a man every inch his equal, one he respected, perhaps even admired.

"I will scout ahead for signs," said the Indian.

"You should rest, if only for a moment or two."

"I will rest when this is done," he said and threw himself over the back of his pony.

Simms watched him trot away, wondering, not for the first time, what drove the scout on. He seemed gripped by such resolve, such determination, almost as if he had some personal interest in finding the train robbers as quickly as possible. Why that should be, Simms couldn't guess, and he drifted over to his horse and gave it a handful of oats to chew on. He checked the carbine, housed in a sheath across the rear of the saddle. Satisfied, he next turned to the little Colt thirty-one caliber Allan Pinkerton had insisted he carry. Simms had adapted a holster for the gun, strapping it around his calf, well concealed, but easily reached when lying on his back. Out here, in the wild, untamed Territories, one never knew when such a contingency might be required.

He sank down next to the little fire, pushing the few, meagre embers around with a twig and gazed into the flames. His eyes grew heavy and he allowed himself to lie back.

Almost at once, he sat up with a start, reaching for his gun, woken by the sound of a breaking branch. Something moved off to his right and he was about to find cover when he saw Deep Water's pony scratching at the ground some way off. Relaxing, Simms went to settle back down when a shape loomed from his left, close like a shadow, as quiet as air. Simms snapped his head around and looked up to see the scout standing not three feet from him. "Jesus," breathed Simms, "you're damned good, I never even…" He grew tense, noting the Indian's concerned expression. "Trouble?"

Deep Water shrugged. "There is the dust of horses. They ride fast, perhaps twenty of them."

"Are they Indians?"

"No. None of my people would ride this way in this heat."

"Very well," said Simms, and he stood up. He crossed to his horse and drew out the carbine from its scabbard. "Let me take a look. You wake Cartwright, but don't spook him none. We don't know who these riders could be. They might even be Mormons, out scouting ahead for more of Johnstone's troopers."

"Mormons would not be a danger, I think. My people have met with them many times. They respect the land, they respect us."

"Bannocks killed some, half a year or more ago. Like I said, not all of your people think the same way as you, so let's just take this nice and easy. Agreed?"

Deep Waters nodded and went over to where Cartwright lay huddled amongst the rocks, whilst Simms found himself a large rock, climbed up to the top and perched himself on it.

He extended the small field telescope he'd taken from one of his saddlebags and scanned the broad, open plain. He slowly scanned from west to east, then snapped his view back to a smudge in the distance. He focused in on what he saw. Riders.

"I'll be damned," he hissed, dropped his hands to his lap and called down to Deep Water, who seemed to be experiencing trouble rousing Cartwright. "By the way they're moving, I'd say they're soldiers. And you were right. I count twenty."

If Deep Water felt pleased about his accurate appraisal, he didn't show it, his face remaining impassive. He turned away and took up shaking Cartwright by the shoulder until the young man stirred, beating away the Indian's hand, complaining loudly, "What the hell is it?"

"Friends," said Simms. He raised the carbine one handed towards the sky, and let off a single shot. The blast boomed out across the plains and Simms checked through his telescope to see if his signal prompted the desired response. Satisfied, he scrambled down the side of the large rock, and when he reached the ground, added through clenched teeth, "At least, I hope they're friends."

The young officer in charge of the troop, fresh-faced and eager looking, saluted stiffly as Simms stepped up close, and stroked the nose of the fine-looking horse on which the man sat.

"Thank you for the signal, sir. I'm Lieutenant Fowler," the officer said. "We received word of your passing. Colonel Johnstone sent a messenger over to the ferry as soon as you arrived at Fort Bridger."

"Well, he's nothing if not efficient. He ordered you to come accompany us?"

"No, sir. We're rotating our tour of duty. Our orders are to check on your safety before returning to Bridger where I shall report and—"

In The Blood

"No need for all the details," said Simms. "Our direction lies to the southwest of the river. We're in pursuit of a bunch of outlaws. I don't suppose you've come across anyone?"

"No sir, no one at all. We're a day out from the ferry and haven't seen a thing. Not even a prairie dog, truth be told. I do not believe I have ever traversed such an empty and God-forsaken land as this."

"Well, it can be a might unforgiving, that's for sure."

"My commanding officer at the Colorado Ferry, Major Calhoon is anxious to be reinforced, so we can't delay." He tipped his hat. "I hope you understand, sir, but now that I see all is well with you, my orders are to—"

"Why is Calhoon so anxious? Has there been any trouble?"

"Not as yet, sir. But Major Calhoon is dismissive of the agreement made between Brigham Young and the President. He says it is nothing more than pigs-swill." He blanched. "Begging your pardon, sir, but those are his words, not mine."

Simms grinned and held up his hand, "I'm sure of that, Lieutenant. Calhoon can be somewhat discourteous with his language, I know that much. What does he think is going to happen?"

"He says the Mormons need to be taught a lesson, sir. My saddlebags contain a formal request to Colonel Johnstone to send more ... *seasoned* troops to help guard the ferry. Other than that, I'm not sure what the Major has in mind."

"Just so long as it doesn't get in the way of my business, I'm not really interested, Lieutenant." Simms paused as Cartwright moved up next to him. The young man brought his heels together and saluted, despite his lack of formal headgear or uniform. Simms gestured towards his young companion. "Allow me to introduce Second-Lieutenant Forrest Cartwright. Lieutenant Cartwright is aiding me in the apprehension of the outlaws."

Fowler studied Cartwright for a moment before extending his hand. Cartwright took it in his left and an awkward moment passed between the two men. "The men we're after shot me through the right arm," explained Cartwright, "after they'd murdered my father in front of my mother's eyes."

"Good God."

"This is more than a manhunt for me, Lieutenant Fowler. It's retribution."

"Yeah, well, we have to catch them first," said Simms.

A dark look came over Fowler's face as he looked beyond the two men to where Deep Water stood, silent, eyes roaming elsewhere. "I see you have a redskin with you. You think that's wise?"

"Finest tracker I've ever known," said Simms evenly.

"There's been some trouble in the direction you're heading," said Fowler, never taking his gaze away from the scout. "Several homesteads have been attacked. Their raiding parties are roaming ever wider, and they are bold, contemptuous of us. Seems any good feeling there once was between settlers and the Indians has well and truly disappeared." He shifted his position in his saddle and pulled a face. "I'd be a might cautious if I were you, sir. You never know when a savage will turn and resort back to type."

"Well, it's *white* savages we're pursuing, Lieutenant. Seems to me that *type* is not limited to the color of a man's skin, more his circumstances."

Fowler stiffened, about to give a response when he caught Deep Water moving closer. Reddening slightly, the Lieutenant gave another salute. "We'll be moving on, sir. I shall give the Colonel your regards."

Simms nodded and stepped aside as Fowler turned in his saddle, arm raised and shouted, "Forward, men," and flicked the reins to take up the lead once more.

"You think it's true, what he says about the raids?" said Cartwright as he stood next to the Pinkerton, both watching the soldiers trundling by. He held a neckerchief to his nose and mouth as dust swirled up in a great cloud.

"Could be," shouted Simms above the thundering of hooves.

As the last of the soldiers cantered out of earshot, Deep Water muttered, "I fear for us all, Pinkerton man. We need to catch these men you pursue quickly, before the whole of this prairie is set alight by the suspicion and hatred of these blue-coats."

"My father always said he believed a greater war was waiting for us," interjected Cartwright, "but I'm not sure what he meant by that."

Simms rubbed his chin as the diminishing clouds of dust dwindled in the late afternoon sun. "I'm no supporter of any kind of war, Lieutenant, but I hope I'm old and grey before the next one starts." He turned and winked. "If I get to be old and grey, that is."

"You think there's a chance you might not?"

"Who can say what awaits any us, especially in a place as cruel and as heartless as this."

"In that case, I'll give up my prayers to ask God Almighty that we're kept alive until we overcome those murdering bastards, for if I go to my grave without having my revenge, I'm likely to come back as a ghost and haunt this place for eternity."

Studying the young man intensely for some moments, Simms at last turned away to squint after the remaining smudges of the troop and wished he too, could find some form of faith strong enough to ask for what he desired most of all. Peace.

Nine

Remnants of violence on the journey west

They made steady progress across the open vastness of the plain, occasional outcrops of rock or sparse patches of vegetation hyphenating the otherwise uniform greyness of the land. Deep Water scouted ahead, often dropping out of sight, but always returning to report on the emptiness awaiting them. Until, on the fourth day, when he rode up with his expression ingrained with concern.

"There is a camp ahead."

Simms shot a glance towards Cartwright, whose back grew rigid, his mouth a thin line, face ashen. "Is it them?" asked the young man.

"No. But there is someone there. A dead man."

The dead man, as the three rolled into the deserted camp, was on his back, eyes wide open, flesh burned black by the unrelenting sun. A gaping hole beneath his left ear, surrounded by congealed blood, told the story of his demise. Buzzards had already started to pick at his remains. He wore a black suit with a waistcoat. A scuffed top hat lay close by. Simms got down from his horse and scraped around what was not so much a camp, as a piece of shaded ground with a fire built in the center. He sampled the cold embers between finger and thumb and looked to Deep Water, who was already studying signs in the dirt.

"It is a wagon, heavy and slow moving. A single horse pulls it and it moves there," he pointed. Simms stood and moved alongside the Indian. He grunted.

Cartwright peered down at the corpse. "Do you think he's one of them?"

Simms shook his head, squeezing Cartwright's arm as he stepped past him. "No. He looks like an undertaker, but whatever he was, he wasn't no outlaw.

Whoever took his wagon, however, may just be." He gave a nod of reassurance. "We may be about to find them."

But what they found, some hours later, was the evidence of yet more violence. This time the signs of tepees were everywhere, proving this was indeed a camp once. Standing forlorn was the wagon, the horse that pulled it long gone. One rotting, half-eaten corpse of a large man lay sprawled in the center. Deep Water studied it. "Shot, by arrow and gun," he mumbled, kicking at the body in disgust. "From what I see, this man jumped down from the wagon and came over here." He pointed to a gnarled, dried-up tree stump. He sauntered over, ran his fingers over the crumbling bark. "Here. Someone was tied to this piece of wood. See," he waved his palm over the ground close by, "his feet, digging into the ground, as if trying to get away."

"Get away from what?" asked Cartwright, his voice sounding small – fearful of the answer perhaps.

"Him, maybe," said Deep Water, nodding at the corpse. "But there are other signs here, of a horse, heavy footprints. A big man, much bigger than this dead one." He released a slow breath. "Then they went. Two horses, riding away yonder, pursued by many others for there," he pointed again, "the tracks of unshod ponies. As we are close to the Trail, I think they could be Shoshone."

"Is that significant?" asked Cartwright with a frown. "Aren't they all the same?" He creased his brow. "Indians, I mean."

Deep Water's eyes flashed, and Simms hurriedly stepped between them. "No. They ain't all the same, Lieutenant. If we follow these signs we'll head into the mountains, and then we're in Ute territory. We'll have them to the north of us, Shoshone to the south. Not a happy place to be, my friend. They hate each other, but they hate us even more. The Trail cut through Shoshone land, and as many headed West because of the lure of gold, trouble sparked all along it. I reckon we ain't seen the last of it. So, we have to be a might careful."

"But, it's them, right?" Cartwright licked his lips, his eyes holding Simms's own, pleading. "The two riders? It's them, the train-robbers, right?"

"It's possible. Reports were of six of them, all told. Five that hit the train, killed your pa and those other passengers. One got himself killed. This one," he nodded to the corpse, "he could well be a second. That leaves four, including the sharpshooter. Could be he came in here, rescued another and the two of them have ridden off to rendezvous with their pals. Might be this is the best bit of good news we've had for a while."

"So, who is this lump of shit?"

"An argument maybe. Who knows, but it is mighty strange they should be spread out as they are."

"Perhaps they argued over their share of the money? Their kind often do."

"That's true enough."

Rolling his tongue over his top lip, Cartwright looked every inch an eager young boy, filled with wonder and expectation. His face creased into a wide, open grin. "Then we've got them, by God!"

Tilting his head, Simms arched a single eyebrow. "Boy, if Shoshone are on their trail too, something bad happened here, something which made them want to run down the two whites. It might be best if we took it easy. Last thing we want to do is step on Native toes."

"I'm damned if I'm going to let a pack of redskins get in the way of me doing what I need to do, Detective Simms."

Sensing Deep Water bristling close by, Simms gritted his teeth and gave Cartwright a withering look. "Boy, you'd best not talk that way when you have one of those people close by."

Cartwright gaped at the Scout. "He's a Shoshone?"

"I am Kiowa," snarled Deep Water, "but whatever I am, I am Redskin. According to you."

Shaking his head, Cartwright expelled his breath, pushed past Simms and hauled himself up into his saddle. "I couldn't give a good damn who the hell he is, or who the hell the others are." He twisted in his saddle and drew out a carbine from the sheath strapped to the left flank of his horse. It was Colt model, with revolving cylinder. He checked its load before using it to point in the direction of the many tracks. "I'm going to find the bastards that shot down my father and kill them. And I ain't taking it easy, Detective."

"Even if you find them, even if you kill them," said Simms slowly, "there are still two more out there somewhere. What about them?"

"Oh, the others will tell me, Detective." He slid the carbine back into its leather holder. "Trust me on that. Are you coming?"

"Like I said; easy."

Cartwright grunted, kicked his horse and took off at a wild ride, heading across the plain, left hand gripping the reins, right hand dangling limply by his side.

"He will get himself killed," said Deep Water.

Simms nodded, squeezing his mouth into a thin line. "And how the hell will I explain that to my bosses?"

"Perhaps then, we should go after him Pinkerton man, and save him from himself."

A tiny snigger, then Simms pulled his coat together and strode over to his horse. "I didn't know you were Kiowa."

"There are many things you do not know about me, Pinkerton man."

Simms nodded, keeping his thoughts unspoken. Not for the first time since sharing life on the trail with this man, the old feelings of impending danger, which were his constant companion during the Mexican War, rumbled around in his gut. As he steered his horse across the plain, he made sure the scout never dropped behind him.

Just in case.

Ten

Death amongst the rocks

For the umpteenth time, he slowed down his horse and turned to look out across the plain. Harris, breathing hard, bent over, face racked with pain, said, "What do you see?"

"Something." The big man reached behind him and groped around inside one of his saddlebags. He uttered a grunt when he retrieved a small pair of field glasses. "Got these off a Prussian associate some years back." He brandished them in front of Harris. "Damn fine things they are too." He put them to his eyes and scanned over the area they'd travelled throughout the long, hot day. He didn't grunt this time, but hissed. "Shit."

Harris perked up, straining his neck to look. "What do you see?"

"Indians."

"Oh Jesus. I told you they'd come, I told you—"

"Shut up," snapped the big man. He turned away and searched the surrounding scrub. Again, he put the field glasses to his eyes, but in the opposite direction this time. "All righty. We have a chance." He looped the strap of the glasses around his neck. "There are some rocks ahead. A hillside, looks too steep to climb right to the top, but there might be cover somewhere up there. That's where we'll hold out."

"But how many could you see?"

"Enough."

"You can't be thinking of fighting them savages? Have you any idea what they'll do to us?"

"That's why we have to fight. They're a fair ways behind us, so we have time. Unless you want to stand around here and snuggle up close to them for a little pow-wow."

"Are you crazy?"

"No, but you are if you think we have any other choice but to kill them. Or die trying." He put his heels to his horse and cantered across to the rocky area he hoped would allow them some advantage over the pursuing Indians.

Finding the way tough going, Harris swore and berated his horse, kicking it fiercely, urging it to move over the rising ground.

"She'll throw you if you ain't careful."

"Damn it to hell," spat Harris and dropped down. He rubbed at his backside as his companion studied him from a few paces away. "I think it's about time you let me in on a few things. Like, who the hell you are, for starters."

"You already know."

"I know Lol hired you for your shootin', and your shootin' is damned good."

"Well, there you are then."

"There has to be something more."

"Name is Talpas. That's all you need to know. Now," he tugged out one of the ivory handled Colts in his waistband and thrust it, butt first, towards Harris. "Find a place to the rear for the horses, then get yourself way over to the left, out of sight. I'll draw them in, hopefully take one or two down before they get too close. When they come within range, you open up with this."

Harris ruminated, breath coming in short, sharp gasps, his eyes settling hungrily on the Colt. "You're trusting me with that?"

"Boy, if we don't work together on this, we're dead. Nothing simpler. Now do as I say. We've got less than half an hour is what I reckon."

Harris nodded and put out a trembling hand to take the revolver. He gazed upon it as if it were some wondrous treasure from a long-forgotten palace. Or tomb. "Is it loaded?"

"Well, it ain't much damned good if it isn't. It has five shots, ready to go." He slid down from his horse and readjusted the frilled, canvas scabbard across his back. He handed Harris the reins to his horse. "I'm gonna find myself a vantage point. Hobble the horses a way off. If they spook, we're done for. Once this is over, we need to get as far away as possible. These bucks won't stop, not after what we've done, so we have to end this here and now. You understand?"

Harris nodded. "What if I miss with my shooting? I've never been all that good."

"Well, you don't wanna miss, so today you'd better make sure you do the very best you can."

Swallowing hard, Harris took the reins, and along with his own horse, led the beasts away from the outcrop. Talpas watched him, then spat out a long line of tobacco juice before he scrambled up the rock face.

The escarpment loomed some thirty feet or more overhead. Talpas studied its hard, sharp surface for some time, thought he spied a way, and set out on his ascent. Within a few moments, he realized the enormity of his task, for the climb proved difficult from the outset. Loose rock, like shale, crumbled away under his hands and feet, forcing him to pause often and long, reassessing his route continuously. By the time he reached a piece of level rock, cut into the face as if by some gigantic pickaxe, the sweat ran down his face like a small waterfall, dripping into his eyes, stinging them. With a loud grunt, he hauled himself over the lip, rolled onto the ledge and lay there, breathing hard. Concentrating on ridding his mind of any doubts or concerns, he stared towards the clear sky, controlling his breathing, settling his nerves. As his body recovered and with his concentration restored, he sat up and took another look through the field glasses. The warriors were moving with an easy arrogance, assured of overcoming their prey. They appeared young, lean, naked bodies burnished by the sun and the lead warrior, much bigger than the rest, seemed to be gazing straight at Talpas.

The sharpshooter lowered the glasses, estimating the distance between him and the approaching bucks. With great care, almost reverence, he unstrapped the canvas scabbard and withdrew his rifle, a Whitworth rifled musket, with an optimum range of 1000 yards. As it was a single-shot, muzzle-loading weapon, he went to it with his usual methodical precision. In normal times. he could fire two good shots every minute, and an especially adapted tripod stand, fitted close to the end of the barrel, aided him in taking the best shot he could.

Every other second, as he loaded up the gun, he took a glance across the plain. They continued to move with a slow, deliberate gait, confident of the outcome, unaware of what awaited them. Four. He pulled out the field glasses and checked. No more than four of them. Dear God, their arrogance was breathtaking and brought a stifled laugh to his throat. In a few short moments, they would be dead and a tiny twinge of regret coursed through him, for they wouldn't realize their folly until it was too late. He longed for them to know, to suffer; to understand death had defeated them. Recognizing the look in a victim's eyes when such knowledge struck home was the thing he relished above all else. The irony being, of course, he rarely got the chance to enjoy those moments, when so many of his kills occurred from long-distance. He sighed, leaned to his right and spat. Far or near, in the final analysis, a killing was a killing, to be savored and his heart fizzled with excitement at the prospect.

A sound from below caused him to jump and he reached for his other Colt Navy. But then he relaxed as he saw Harris worming his way over a cluster of large boulders, squeezing himself between them. From this distance, Talpas couldn't make out the man's expression, but he felt sure it was one of absolute terror. Harris had probably already wet himself, pathetic sap that he was. What was Lol thinking when he hired him and the rest of that bunch of no-hopers? The only one worth a bean was the half-breed, Chato. As dangerous and cunning an individual as Talpas had ever come across, and he had come across many.

He remembered how he'd ridden into the tumbledown town of Benediction one fateful Sunday afternoon, riding hard out of Hope Valley with a posse of hard-drinking bastards on his trail. The council from the neighboring town of Glory hired him to take out a bunch of Indians who were raiding some of the outlying homesteads in the area, but his last shot had blown off the head of Judge Jeremiah Malpas. The locals didn't take too kindly to the accident, blaming Talpas for shooting the old judge on purpose. Of course, they used the incident as an excuse not to pay him. When he'd killed the last of his pursuers and walked into the saloon bar in Benediction, an old timer in the corner whistled in admiration at the sight of the Whitworth. "Good God Almighty, what a magnificent weapon that is." He waddled over, his rheumy eyes taking in the lines of the rifle and he whistled again. "I am something of a marksman myself, sir, although you would not think so now, to look at me."

"You recognise this gun?"

"I do indeed, sir. Of British design and manufacture. A magnificent gun. A gun of the future."

"I'm impressed by your knowledge."

"I myself used Enfields, but their range was nothing as compared to this. Why, my marks could see the color of my eyes by the time they were in range."

"So, you're a sharpshooter."

"Was. Three years ago, damned rifle misfired, blew off my first two fingers." He showed his hand to confirm his words. "Since then, all I've got are my memories."

"I'd like to buy you a drink, sir. Seems we have much in common."

"We regulators should stick together, especially with times being so hard."

"Indeed we should." And he thrust out his hand. "I'm pleased to know you."

The old-timer grinned. "Beaudelaire Talpas, at your service."

The service proved most beneficial, as some hours later, with night covering them all, he helped a very drunken Talpas out of the saloon, took him down a side alley and put his Bowie knife into the old man, burying it deep. He then put the body over the back of his horse and rode out of town, putting a good couple of miles between himself and Benediction. He buried the old man in a shallow pit, stuffing some of his own personal papers inside the dead man's vest. Any one from Glory wishing to find Ishmael Farage would be sadly disappointed, for Farage was now dead, buried in this cold and lonely place. He covered the body over, and satisfied, rode on. Three days later, entering yet another half-constructed mining town, he signed up again to kill hostile Indians, only this time he signed under his new identity; Beaudelaire Talpas.

The memory blurred and he concentrated on the present. Taking a deep breath, he wiped his brow with the back of his hand, then settled down behind the rear sight of the rifle.

The Indians were close now, slowing down to a walk, the lead warrior leaning over the neck of his pony, peering at the ground. Something caused him to pull up sharply and he raised his right arm. The others drew close, and as they all studied the ground, Talpas shot the second in line clean through the head, blowing off the top of his skull.

In an instant, the others bolted in every direction, trying to keep clear of the area and Talpas set to reloading his rifle. Below him, the crack of a revolver split the hot air and Talpas grinned. Harris had proved his mettle. Whether he survived the firefight or not, he'd given Talpas a few valuable moments.

As he worked the ramrod to press home the lead ball, he chanced a look to the foot of the escarpment and saw the three Indians scurrying over the rocks and larger boulders. He saw Harris standing, aiming with infinite care. Heard the discharge, saw the Indian fall. But the next one was already closing fast, his arms streaking out, an awful scream emitting from his throat. He hit Harris hard and they fell together in a tangle of arms and legs.

Deliberately, Talpas aimed the rifle towards where the third Indian crouched down behind a boulder. He'd seen the Indian duck down not seconds ago, so now he waited for him to show. Time wasn't on his side, for he felt certain Harris would be unable to overcome his assailant. The seconds stretched out into seeming eternity, but Talpas did not falter. He held his breath, knew his patience would bring its reward. And when it did and the Indian jumped up, the shot took the warrior full in the chest, blowing him backwards across the scree.

Without a pause, Talpas put aside his rifle and scrambled down the rock face. He slipped and stumbled, landed on his backside and allowed himself to slide all the way down to the bottom. As he went, he pulled out the Colt, and as soon as he hit level ground, he vaulted over the rocks and saw the remaining Indian with a hatchet, about to cleave open Harris's head. He raised the Navy and put two bullets into the Indian assailant.

The sound of the blast echoed across the scorched land but nothing else made a noise, nor moved. Nothing else dared to do so. Talpas stood, rooted to the ground, straight-backed, listening. The tiniest of moans, from somewhere to his right and he moved towards it, saw the Indian he'd shot in the chest. The wound was bad, incapacitating, but Talpas wasn't about to gamble. He took aim and put a round between the man's eyes and it was over.

They were all dead.

"Holy Mother," breathed Harris, bent double, wheezing with pain and disbelief. "I never thought I could do it. Never, not in a million years."

"Well, you did," said Talpas, moving towards him

"My wrists hurt like sin, my throat is as dry as this here earth, and that bastard would have killed me if you hadn't…" He brought his face up and looked at his savior. "Thank you. You saved my life."

"Like I said. We're in this together." He motioned towards the dead. "I doubt if there'll be more of them, not after this, although I'm thinking we should never cross this way again."

"By God, you are one helluva shot. I know you killed the guard in the train, but sweet Jesus… I've never seen anything like this."

"That guard, he was a mistake." He laughed at Harris's bewildered, startled look. "I was meant to shoot the brake man."

"Well, I'm grateful you made no mistakes today." Harris shook his head. "I'm sorry for not trusting you before, but…" He shrugged and handed over his empty Colt Navy. "Those doubts, they've all gone now, after what you did, so

I'm going to tell you." His face twisted into a grimace as he stretched his back, then took to gently massaging his own wrist. Talpas waited. "Lol, he had a second meeting place, if something prevented him from getting to our hideout. The Silver Dime Saloon, in the town of Buryridge. It's a mining town, still doing a little business. Rumor has it someone found a silver-lode, gave the town something of a boost."

"Buryridge? Sounds a delightful place."

"It's a filthy hole, that's what it is, but Lol said he'd head there and give us ten days. *Ten*, Mr. Talpas."

"He's on his own?"

"I'm guessing there'll be only one other left now, after you did for old Ned back at the Injun camp."

"That'll be Chato."

Harris shrugged. "The half-breed?" Talpas grunted and put the empty Navy into his waistband and Harris continued. "He might be alive still. He was a wily old goat. Dangerous, too."

"Well, I guess we'd better be making our way over to this Burybridge and hope dear old Lol is of a mind to hand over our share."

"No reason why he shouldn't. I was making my way there when I became somewhat detoured."

"Oh? Was that your little altercation with the savages?"

"I found a squaw on my way, taking water from a river. Man, she was a honey. So, I made her acquaintance."

Talpas frowned. "You mean...?"

Harris chuckled. "It's something of a weakness of mine. Almost cost me my life. She wrestled me to the ground, made a grab for my revolver and in the struggle, it went off."

"You killed her?"

"Pure accident, I swear to God. But, as I made to get the hell away, a swarm of bucks came upon me as if out of thin air. Dear God, they was angry!" He chuckled again. "They beat the living shit out of me, then dragged me back to their camp. Their plan was to cut off my balls and roast them in a pot. Least ways, that was what the big fella said. Him there." Harris pointed to where the huge leader of the warriors lay sprawled across the blood-soaked ground. "They went off hunting, giving me time to think well on what they would do on their return. Ned came across me, driving that damned wagon, pretending to be some sort of preacher. You know the rest."

"Indeed I do, excepting the direction of this town you said."

"Buryridge?" Harris grinned, and pointed vaguely to the west. "A day's ride. We'll pick up the trail once we clear these hills." He grew quiet, his face losing its previous amusement. "What if Lol won't do what's right. What if he won't give us our due?"

"Then I'll kill him."

"That might not be so easy. If Chato is with him, he's deadlier than a rattler."

"He is." Talpas grinned. "But so am I."

Harris nodded, casting his eye across the rocks and the dead Indians. "A truer word ain't ever been spoken, I reckon."

"Thank you, Harris."

"Thank *me*? You ain't got nothing to thank me for, Mr. Talpas. Nothing at all."

"Your trust. Your honesty. For that I thank you."

He smiled and saw Harris's face redden slightly as he blushed with embarrassment.

Then Talpas turned the Navy Colt on him and shot Harris through the gut.

Eleven

Information from dying lips

"We got to keep moving," said Simms, after the sound of gunfire echoing across the open vastness brought him up sharp. "If that boy has got himself killed, then I'm truly in the shit."

Deep Water shrugged, turning to the west. "I see no other tracks but the four ponies. I think the boy has ridden yonder." He gestured towards the west.

"But do you see his tracks?"

"Not yet. But I will."

Simms pulled in a long breath. "I wonder where the hell he's gone?"

"If he stays out on the open range, he will die within two days in this heat. Perhaps less."

"You're full of comfort, Deep Water. Thanks." Simms bit his lip, struggling to decide what to do. The sense of dread, which had haunted him these past few days, continued to scratch away at him. He stood up in his stirrups, stretching out his legs, then settled back into his saddle. "All right, you head west, and pick up his trail. I shall head for those hills yonder."

"From where the shooting comes?" Deep Water shook his head. "The Shoshone warriors will kill you, Pinkerton man."

"This may surprise you, but I don't kill that easy."

"Best if I go and speak with them and you follow the boy. That way we will both live."

Simms frowned. "And if I don't find him? I'm no tracker."

"You will find him, I am certain of it."

"Really?" Simms wasn't convinced. The notion that there was more to the scout than he was telling once more gnawed away at Simms, troubling him. Troubling him more than anything else, causing his anxiety to increase. "Is there something you ain't telling me, Deep Water?"

The scout looked away. Was it his usual reluctance to hold another's gaze, or was there another reason? "There is nothing to tell."

"You seem mighty anxious to get to those Shoshones. Or maybe it's the men the Shoshone are in pursuit of you wish to meet up with?"

The scout kept his face turned away. "You are mistaken, Pinkerton man."

"Am I? I wonder."

Deep Water finally turned around, his face impassive as always. "I shall go and speak with the Shoshone warriors. If you take a slow route to the west, I shall catch you within the hour."

"All right," said Simms, trying to keep the reluctance out of his voice. "I'll go, real steady. You set off, as fast as you can. All being well, we'll meet up in the course of the next day."

Deep Water took the hint and whirled around, faster than he'd moved since the first moment Simms met him. Striking the rump of his pony with the flat of his hand, Deep Water pounded away towards the cluster of hills far off on the horizon. Simms gazed after him, wondering if he should have pressed the scout further, forced out the truth and dispelled the fears rumbling away inside.

Reluctantly, he turned his horse to the west, trying to push away his concerns.

But he failed to do so.

* * *

Crouching amongst a clump of dried and tangled gorse, Cartwright trembled uncontrollably. From the short distance that separated him from the nearby hills, he witnessed how the Indians had died. What terrified him most were the actions of the large man with the long hair, the almost casual way he dispatched the four warriors and how he spoke then shot the other white man. This man, who slumped between the rocks with his life's blood bubbling over his grasping fingers, howled so horribly that Cartwright almost vomited in terror. Instead, he flattened himself into the ground, hands pressed over his ears, and waited, biting down his sobs. Only when the pounding of a retreating horse filtered through his fear did he chance to look.

He waited. The stricken man's cries lessened, but just as Cartwright decided it was safe enough to investigate further, the sound of a rapidly approaching horse caused him to return to the gorse and hide again.

It was Deep Water. Even before his pony came to a halt, the scout was jumping from the animal's back. In his hand was a carbine and he was running at a crouch, head moving from side to side. He reached a large rock and crouched behind it. Cartwright watched, fascinated, as Deep Water made his way with extreme caution to where the wounded man lay. A brief exchange of words, another scan of his surroundings, and Deep Water was returning to his horse, vaulting onto it, and smacking its rump with the rifle. The pony broke into a mad gallop and Cartwright again waited until the receding dust was nothing but a smudge in the distance before he moved.

Grimacing, he examined his bare arms and the many scratches caused by the brittle gorse. He picked out almost a dozen sharp barbs from his flesh, gave his right arm a brusque rub and wished he could do the same for his left. For the thousandth time, he cursed the man who'd shot him, and with a heavy tread, made his way to where he'd tied his horse amongst several withered trees way off to his right. The horse snickered at his approach, and he calmed it with a gentle rub of its nose, loosened the rein from around the tree and made to walk the horse back towards the rocks. His heart almost stopped when he saw Simms sitting astride his own mount, barring his way.

Swallowing hard, Cartwright's eyes fell to the detective's horse, and the pieces of canvas tied around its hooves. And Simms sat, his head tilted, an expectant expression on his face, silent and grim, waiting for an explanation, as a patient father might a naughty child.

For his part, Cartwright – mouth open, eyes wide with shock – could offer nothing in return. Sighing deeply, Simms dropped down from his horse and motioned towards the canvas-covered hooves, which helped keep his approach relatively unnoticed. "Don't be thinking this was for your benefit. Did you see where Deep Water went to?"

Something flickered across Cartwright's eyes, a recognition Simms was addressing him, a realization he was required to speak. His only offering was a slight shrug of the shoulders.

"What in the name of hell were you thinking of doing over here, son?"

"I… I don't know. Something."

"Something which may have gotten you killed."

"I didn't think and I…" He averted his eyes, his face growing red.

"And what happened over there?" Simms motioned across to the hillside.

"Killing."

A single word, but containing more terror than an entire soliloquy. Simms nodded and grunted. "All right, you uncover my horse's hooves then bring her and your own over to those rocks. I'll go take a look." He pulled the Colt Dragoon from its holster.

"He's gone."

Simms stopped in mid-stride. "Who? Deep Water?"

"Yes, him too. But I meant the killer. I saw him. Jesus, I've never seen anything like it."

"You want to tell me about it?"

Cartwright looked pained, forced a single shake of the head, then looked away, more in shame than anything else. "Maybe later."

Simms didn't press him. The violence he'd witnessed undoubtedly reawakened the killing of his own father and the subsequent horrors such an atrocity imbued. So the detective turned away and moved cautiously towards the rocks.

He found the wounded man almost as soon as he reached the first outcrop. There were other bodies, of course. The Shoshone warriors. All dead, all shot, two sporting enormous wounds in head and chest. The wounded man, murmuring constantly, lay in a crevasse between the rocks, blood drooling from his mouth. He whimpered more loudly as his eyes locked on Simms and the revolver in his hand. He attempted to scramble further backwards, but only succeeded in creating more agony for himself, his face creasing up, hands clutching at the blood-drenched wound in his stomach.

"I can't save you friend," said Simms, squatting down next to the man, studying the gunshot. "I can promise you a decent burial, with prayers said over you. That might help some as you step into the next world."

"It was him that did it, the bastard," gargled the man.

"Indian?"

He shook his head, wincing with the effort. "Talpas."

For a moment, Simms sat rock still, stunned by this revelation. "Talpas? Beaudelaire Talpas, the regulator?"

"A murdering sonofabitch is what he is … Oh dear Christ, it hurts." To give weight to his words, both sets of fingers delved into the wound, as if attempting to rip out the cause of his suffering. "Water. Please. A drink of water."

"I'll give it you, friend. Where did he go, this Talpas?"

"To town. Burybridge. He's gonna meet up with Lol. Get the money."

"Holy shit." Simms craned his neck to see Cartwright plodding across the dirt, leading the two horses. He raised his voice, "Bring me some water." He looked again at the man, reached out and squeezed his shoulder. "Tell me your name, friend. I'll make sure it goes on the cross."

"Harris. Jed Harris. I never meant to do the things I done, I swear to God. But that squaw, she was so pretty. I never seen…" A sudden stab of pain lanced through him and he pitched over to his right, crying out, "Oh God … God, I'm dying. He did this to make me suffer, I know it. Damn him."

"So you were part of the gang that held up the train, is that it? And this Lol, he's one of them?" The wounded man nodded, moaning as Cartwright's shadow fell over them both. Simms peered up, squinting at his companion. "You have the water."

"Damned if I'll give him any."

"Just to ease his passage to the next—"

"Damned I'll give him anything but a bullet in the brain! I heard what he said. The rest of them, they're in that town. Burybridge."

"We don't know much about anything, yet. Give him some more time and a drink of water, then we'll—"

Cartwright gave a sharp cackle of laughter and Simms, confused, turned to look at the wounded Harris again. He grew silent as he stared into those wide-open eyes, realizing no further information would be forthcoming from Harris's mouth ever again.

Twelve

The town of Burybridge

The wooden bridge from which the town took its name, its boards warped and splintered, straddled a dried-up riverbed. Beyond, and a little to the right, lay a sprawl of old and gnarled wooden crosses, markers for the graves of the long forgotten. And further away, at the end of a rutted track, the town itself. Talpas, sitting astride his horse on his side of the long dead river, decided it best to dismount, fearing the bridge might collapse under the combined weight of horse and rider. Before doing so, he pulled out the German field glasses and took a moment to study the nearby town, a ramshackle collection of dilapidated buildings spread along three streets. Most appeared covered with dust, doors half-open on broken hinges, empty windows, flaking paintwork; all sure signs they were no longer in use. A sorry sight, often repeated across the Territory as miners dwindled away from spent local gold and silver lodes. As the veins of precious metals dried up, so did the need for workers. The more vicious took to hiring themselves out as gun hands, to shoot and kill wandering bands of Indians. Most of the Indians were hunting parties, searching out buffalo or other game to fill the bellies of their starving families. Mine owners didn't see it that way and preferred not to take any chances and already the West buzzed with stories of violent red-men, intent on killing anyone who crossed their land. Exaggerations, lies, distortions – none of it mattered to the gun hands so long as they were paid. And in response, the Natives became the very thing the whites believed they were anyway: killers and savages.

Sliding down from his horse, Talpas rolled his big shoulders, repositioning the rifle slung across his back. The sun burned deep, his neck wet with sweat, his buckskin jacket sticking to his skin. What he longed for most of all was a soothing bath; to put his head back, close his eyes and drift. He couldn't remember the last time he felt clean or changed his clothes. He knew he would have to wait, however, for he still had some work to do.

With great care, he led his horse across the bridge, pausing every other step as the tired old boards beneath his feet creaked and groaned horribly. Every now and then, he peered down to the riverbed, a drop of some twelve or so feet. Not a huge fall if the ancient timbers gave way, but enough to break his horse's legs. He looked towards the town again, wondering what awaited him there, if he made it. And as he took another step, he very nearly didn't. An ancient plank splintered and broke with the sharp retort of a rifle shot and he stumbled, his foot dropping through the paper-thin timber. Crying out, he floundered, palms out, pressing down upon the next slatted board and he managed to wriggle free. The horse, spooked, pulled violently against his grip on the reins and for one terrible moment, he believed she would break free. He held on, cursing, but battling to keep calm. If the mare bolted, all would be lost.

He yanked his foot free from the remains of the slat and stood up, stroking the mare's nose, calming her as best he could. The bridge swayed alarmingly but for the time being, it seemed it would hold. Swallowing down his worries, he moved on, balancing himself on his toes, as if that would help.

As he finally stepped off onto the far side, Talpas let out a long breath, forcing himself to relax. The horse, its eyes wide, seemed to share in his relief, and shook itself, releasing a loud whinny. Smiling, Talpas, cradled the mare's head before chancing a glance towards the old bridge, marveling that it continued to straddle the gap of the river. He wondered if another pathway existed across, but if one did it was nowhere in sight. He'd ridden non-stop for hours, right through the night, putting as much distance as possible between himself and the dead Indians, without killing his horse in the process. Now close to his goal, he was damned if any other redskins were going to overtake him before he took what was rightfully his – a share of the money promised to him by Lol. Pulling in a breath, he led the mare some distance away before returning to the bridge to take up an assault on the closest supporting post, working at it with his great arms, loosening the timber from where it sank into the crumbling earth. The wooden slats, across which he moved so gingerly, shivered and shook, the entire structure swaying from side to side. With the sweat rolling down his brow to drip into his eyes, he struggled on, pushing and pulling with all his considerable strength. Gritting his teeth, nothing could distract him, not now his mind was set. Grunting, he spurred himself on, cursing loudly that the structure proved to not be as rickety as he'd first believed.

Just as he was about to give up, one of the slats parted from its companions in a loud crack, and it fell and smashed against the rocks below. Talpas almost let out a high-pitched whoop, delighted his endeavors had paid off so handsomely. A chain-reaction swiftly followed, other planks springing free from their dried and frayed restraining ropes, which snapped like whip cracks. He stepped back, hands on hips, gulping in air, his face splitting with a maniacal grin as the bridge gave out one last yawning protest and crumbled in a great shattered heap into the earth below, sending up a cloud of dust. As it settled, Talpas allowed himself a moment of self-congratulation for now, anyone following would have to find an alternative crossing. And that would give him more than time enough to seek out and confront Lol.

Stepping out from the dim, depressed confines of the 'Silver Dime' saloon, Lol put his fists into the small of his back and stretched out his spine. A few joints cracked and he shook himself, letting out a sigh of relief. Sitting down for the best part of three hours, poring over yet another worthless hand of cards, did nothing for his demeanor – physically or mentally. He was close to the limits of his patience and chided himself for agreeing to wait ten days for the rest of the gang to arrive. A week would have been time enough, and this God-awful joke of a town would be nothing but a bad memory by now. Still, he thought to himself with something of a smile, good fortune had brought him together with Spiro and his kid brother Dwayne. The snippet of news they brought to the table whetted Lol's appetite for another robbery, regardless of Chato's reservations. Chato, who stepped up next to him, rolling himself a cigarette, always proved the voice of reason. The wily Mexican stood in silence, paying close attention to laying the tobacco neatly along the paper. "I still don't like it," he said.

"You don't like anything."

"True, but even so, we have enough money to last us—"

"A month? Six weeks?"

"Longer if we are careful."

Lol shook his head, hawked and spat into the dirt on the far side of the boardwalk. "Nah, we're never careful. I've already lost best part of five hundred dollars on cards."

"You told us there was tens of thousands of dollars on that train. Three thousand was all there was in that safe. That's less than we're wanted for on the reward posters."

"So, you going to kill me, earn your money that way, is that it? Shoot me in the back and claim the reward?"

Chato shrugged, ran his tongue along the gummed edge of the paper and put it into his mouth. "Perhaps. I sure as hell don't want to rob another train, not if the pickings are so thin." He fished out a match from a small tin box and struck it along the ribbed side. The match flared and he put the flame to the end of his cigarette and blew out a long trail of smoke. "Besides, we have to wait for the others."

"They're dead."

"How do you know? You have the power of prophesy now?"

Lol frowned at the squat Mexican with his flat, bronzed face, the livid scar running from the corner of his mouth to his eye. It seemed to glow a very vivid red at that moment. "Just a feeling."

"The same feeling you had about how much was on that train?"

"I had it on good authority that miners were waiting in their camp for their wages. I figured—"

"You figured the train would be bringing it to them?" Lol nodded and Chato clicked his tongue. "And now you wish us to act on more hearsay, this time from two drifters who look and smell like they've been on the trail for a few hundred years."

"It ain't hearsay. They brought a message, from the same—"

Chato held up his hand. "Don't tell me – from the same *good authority* who told you about the first load of cash?" Lol grunted and gave a nod. Chato turned away and blew out a stream of smoke. "I think it's bullshit."

"Why would anyone lie?"

"Think about it, my friend. Maybe it is they who want to shoot us, or have been ordered to do so, and claim the reward for themselves? We were wanted men before the robbery, imagine how much the reward for us will be now."

Lol stared at the Mexican for a long time, accepting the plausibility of his words. But he couldn't believe Spiro and his brother would be capable of killing. They were simply not equipped to be successful bounty hunters. Young, gangly and desperate, Lol doubted they'd ever fired their revolvers in anger. "They're not killers."

"Any man can kill if he is hungry enough. I have seen it many times, my friend."

"Yeah, but you've survived."

Chato screwed up his mouth and nodded with a degree of self-satisfaction. "True. I remember those two bounty-hunters who broke into my room as I was rolling around with that whore down in Franklin at Coons' Rancho." He chuckled, drawing deeply on the cigarette. "The look on their faces when they saw me with my Baby Dragoon."

"Is that what the whore called it?"

Chato frowned in puzzlement, then realizing the meaning of Lol's words, burst into laughter. "That is what she said, yes, that damned whore! Before I shot her too." He continued to chuckle with the memory. "Good days, my friend. Happy times. I cannot remember the last time I laughed, spent some moments of tenderness with a whore." He grew silent, deep in thought as he stared at the burning end of his cigarette. "This plan, to take another train… You say you have a feeling, well I do too – and it is one of disaster, my friend. Those two, I doubt they can even piss straight, let alone fire their guns. It will all end in a crisis I think."

"We have little choice. I'm sorry about the paltry amount of money we took last time, I truly am, but I believe it was a genuine mistake, on the part of my contact."

"This is someone you trust? How can you think that after what happened?"

"God damn it, Chato, we *need* to take risks. That's part of our profession."

"Is that what you call it now? A profession?"

Lol gave a short laugh and watched Chato's cigarette fly through the air, to land in the dusty street and instantly die. "Listen, if it goes wrong this time, I'll end it for my contact, I promise you that much."

"Who is he?"

"I can't say, not yet."

"A man of mystery, eh? Just like you, my friend. You keep secrets and I do not like that."

"I've always done what I think best for us, you know that. You know you can trust me."

They held one another's stare. "All right," said Chato at last, his voice resigned, weary. "We do it. But afterwards, we head down to Mexico and relax a little."

"Agreed," said Lol and turned around to face the saloon entrance.

Standing in the doorway, leaning on the double swing doors, was a long streak of a man, a pork-pie hat set at a jaunty angle on his ochre colored hair. His green eyes were set impossibly close, giving him a wild, disturbing look.

"I heard what you said," he drawled, glaring straight towards Chato, and stepped out into the daylight. His blue checked shirt hung out of his trousers, a gunbelt pulled tight around his waist, the holster hanging low on his hip. "You got some doubts about me, breed?"

Chato stiffened and Lol thrust out a restraining arm. "Now, hold up there, Spiro…"

But the young man didn't falter. "You want to see me shoot, you just go right ahead and ask."

"Spiro," said Lol, voice low and controlled, "Chato was only fooling around. Best if we just—"

"Best if he just apologizes, seeing as I resent disparaging remarks."

Lol blinked. "Spiro, you're clearly an educated man, so why don't you—"

"Why don't *he* apologize."

Chato breathed a long sigh. "Why don't you just kiss my ass."

Spiro's expression changed, his mouth growing tighter, eyes flashing. He made a grab for his gun, but Chato took him by surprise, crossing the space between them in a stride. His left hand clamped around Spiro's gun hand, and his right fist smacked into the young man's jaw with tremendous power, sending him reeling back through the swing doors and into the saloon, where he dropped to his knees, stunned. Rushing forward, the Mexican swung a kick into Spiro's jaw and the fight was over.

Following close behind, Lol took it all in within a few seconds; Spiro groaning on the floor, his brother coming up out of his chair, Chato's gun pressing against Dwayne's forehead. The others in the bar, a few worn out old mineworkers, looked on in silence.

Chato glared into Dwayne's quivering face. "Now you tell your brother, if he ever tries to pull a gun on me again, he dies. And you too. You understand?" Chato eased back the hammer and Dwayne squealed and defecated himself.

"Oh sweet Jesus," said Lol, turning away with his hand clamped across his nose, "that stinks, you dirty bastard."

From behind the counter, the balding barkeeper, dressed in faded dungarees and a sweat-stained vest, stepped forward, a double-barreled shotgun in his hands. "I'll have no gunplay here. God knows there's been enough of that."

"No gunplay," said Chato, without turning away from the whimpering Dwayne. "You tell your brother what I said, when he can stand up again, *comprenda*, you little shit?"

The young man nodded, his face a perfect mask of misery, and he quickly scuttled away, leaving the room, heading towards a door in the far corner. Chato watched him go, then turned a quizzical eye to the barman. "If you don't want that rammed up your hairy ass, I'd advise you to put it away."

The barman blanched, looked away and lowered the gun. "Sorry, but I…" He forced a smile, shrugged, and trudged back to the bar.

Lol went over to a nearby table and scooped up a half-empty glass of whisky. He downed it in one. "You sure have a subtle way of putting your feelings across."

"He's lucky I didn't kill him," said the Mexican, studying the semi-conscious Spiro sprawled on the floor. "Perhaps I should have done, and put paid to this miserable idea you have for robbing the train."

"We've agreed. When this little shit can, we'll find out what more he knows, then we can head out and leave this miserable place for good."

Chato grunted and slipped his gun back into its holster. "And never to return." He winked. "At least, not with these two."

Thirteen

In the Silver Dime saloon

From his viewpoint on a raised mound, Talpas levelled his field glasses on the receding shapes of four riders, making their way slowly out of the town. He sucked in air through his teeth and wished he had more chewing tobacco. It helped him think, for now he was in two minds. Whether to continue following and risk being spotted, or wait, then try to pick up their trail. Tracking was never a strong point of his, so he decided to take a gamble, ride into town and find out if anyone knew where the gang's destination might be. Because four men constituted a gang, and he wondered who the new additions might be. Lol always did have a gift for attracting the more questionable individuals in any community. Perhaps he'd hit the mark yet again.

Taking his time, Talpas took his horse into town at a canter. Sitting ramrod straight in the saddle, from the corner of his eyes he noted the many silent, sullen faces staring from behind windows and doorways and several from armed men standing on the boardwalks on either side of the main street. On reaching the saloon, he swung down from his horse and looped the reins over the hitching rail. He rolled his shoulders, slipped his rifle in its sheath from his back and took the steps leading to the swing doors with deliberate slowness, aware of the eyes of the townsfolk boring into his back.

The man behind the counter looked up and two other drinkers standing close by stopped and stared. Giving the interior a cursory glance, Talpas moved easily across the room, nodded his greeting to the others, and laid his rifle across the bar. "I'll have a whisky," he said and placed a few coins next to his sheathed weapon, "followed by a beer."

Scooping up the money without a word, the barman filled a small glass and pushed it towards Talpas who lifted it, breathed in the aroma, then downed it. He smacked his lips and gasped. "Obliged."

The barman filled a tall glass with frothy beer and put it down next to the rifle. "Been out on the trail long?"

"Too long." Talpas sipped his drink, turned, and leaned against the counter, allowing his eyes to settle on a nearby table with playing cards and empty glasses spread over the top. "Someone lose at cards?"

"Nope."

Talpas nodded, craned his neck towards the two men close by. "Are you the gambling men?"

"We're taking our break from the new mine," said one of them, a round, burly looking individual who sprouted a fine thatch of hair from both ears. He had little on top.

"Ah. New mine. Silver, I hear."

"What of it?"

Talpas shrugged. "Just asking. The men who were here, at the table, do you happen to know where they went?"

"Are you a friend of theirs?" asked the barman, his voice growing less friendly and Talpas hung his head and let out a slow, long breath. "Because if you are, you're about as welcome here as yellow fever, mister."

"No, no. I'm not a friend." He turned around, and smiling, tapped his rifle with the fingers of his left hand. He took another sip of beer. "I'm a regulator, charged with introducing those bastards to their maker."

Almost at once, the atmosphere changed and the two men coughed and shuffled nervously, stepping away. The barman swallowed hard. "A regulator?"

Talpas nodded. "Them bastards robbed a train, killed some innocent people. Jeremiah Lomax, across at the Lomax Mining Company, has instructed me to hunt them down."

"I ain't never heard of no Jeremiah Lomax. Who the hell is—"

Talpas cut him off with a raised hand. "No matter. I've been following the gang for days and thought I saw some riders leaving here. But what's curious is, they were four. As I've already shot and killed three of them bastards out of an original five, I'm kind of curious who these new recruits are. Perhaps you could enlighten me?"

"They were here for a few days after coming in from the prairie, that's all I know."

"All of them came in together?"

"No, the two skinny ones, they rode in only yesterday."

"And who might they be?"

"I've no idea. All I know is they soon got might friendly with the others. But, I didn't take to noting the details. Like I said, I tend to keep my nose out of other people's business."

Nodding, Talpas turned his gaze towards the two men, whose faces were now ashen, all their former brevity and brashness gone. "And how about you? You know anything at all about those two boys?"

"We know nothin', saw nothin' too."

"Seems a might strange, you being here in the saloon with them sitting right in front of you." The two miners exchanged a look, full of anxiety and Talpas chuckled softly. "You'd best tell me what I need to know," he said, drawing back his coat to reveal the ivory handle of one of his Colt Navy's. "I've kind of lost my patience, having been out in the sun so long. So just tell me, then you can get back to doing what you do. Whatever that is."

"We're miners. Just like them two boys."

"Ah. So you do know them?"

"Kind of. They got into a fight with one of the team bosses, so they got thrown out. One of 'em, the older one, always had his head in a book. The other, all he did was cackle and grin. Like an idiot."

"Their names?"

"Spiro, I think. But I don't recall the other."

"Spiro Mullaghan," piped up the second miner, "and his brother. Dean or Dwayne or something. Spiro fancied himself as something of a scholar, as well as a gunfighter. I guess they must have teamed up with the ones you're after."

Pulling a face, Talpas looked again at the barman. "So, mister I-don't-stick-my-nose-into-others-business, what did you hear them talk about?"

"I told you, I don't—"

"Yeah, I know what you *told* me, but I have yet to meet a barkeep who doesn't listen in to every other person's conversations, so I'll ask you again. Real nice. What did they talk about?"

The barman spread out his hands and was about to speak when a gun materialized in Talpas' hand as if out of the air, and the big regulator pointed it directly towards the barman's face. "You tell me, or I'll drop you where you stand."

So the barman told him, in a mad rush. All about the plan to rob a train, a train coming out of Fort Bridger, along the new line. A train due in three days. And they'd fought, these men. Some disagreement. The Mexican pulled a gun, after having beaten the one called Spiro half to death. But they went off together and they looked focused, mean.

"They're fixing to rob another train?" Talpas tried to keep the disappointment out of his voice, but he failed. The miserable bunch had spent all the money, including his share. And it had been a tidy sum. He recalled Lol telling them all, sitting there in the cantina, swilling whisky with a honey-thighed whore sitting on his lap nibbling his ear. *"Ten thousand at least,"* he'd barked. *"Maybe even twenty! Hot damn, we're gonna be rich."* Well, rich they weren't. And now they were off to try their luck again. Talpas sighed and put his Navy Colt away. "Thank you kindly for all your help. I'll be having another whisky, then I'll be on my way." He finished his beer and smiled.

The footfalls of the men coming through the door almost caused him to spin and pull out his guns once again, but he already knew it was too late. He turned his head with extreme slowness and noted they all had carbines, and the one in the center sported a sheriff's badge on his shirt.

"And you'll be Beaudelaire Talpas, I'm thinking," said the sheriff and Talpas closed his eyes and groaned.

Fourteen

Words spoken for the dead … and some for the living

They buried Harris as Simms promised. The Pinkerton, with his hat clutched in both hands, lowered his head whilst Cartwright spoke some words. Words which Simms neither listened to, nor cared about. Any faith he may have once harbored lay abandoned on the battlefields of the Mexican War. Ten years ago, Simms took off his United States Army uniform for the last time, and with it, any lingering belief in a compassionate god. He rarely thought of such things now, except when circumstance called for a comforting word to ease another's suffering. Since joining the ranks of the Pinkerton Detective Agency, such words were often repeated. But he uttered them without thought, a mechanical response, nothing more. And so, as Cartwright prayed, he turned his mind to the sharpshooter whose bullets tore into the Shoshone assailants. There could be little doubt it was the same killer who shot the guard on the train. As to his identity, and the accuracy of his shooting, Simms was more convinced than ever it had to be Ishmael Farage. Harris revealed, before dying, the name of the killer was Beaudelaire Talpas. Perhaps this was an alias, a way to confuse the authorities. Whatever the real killer's true identity was, as a consequence the pursuit would need to be cautious in the extreme, for a quarry with such immense talent for long-range killing was one of the most dangerous to confront.

"Amen."

Simms looked up to see Cartwright fitting his hat on his head. He caught Simms's look and his eyes narrowed.

"I did not want to do that."

"I know. But thank you anyway."

"You're a strange one, Detective. You promise the man you'll bury him, but you weren't willing to say a prayer."

"I have my reasons. Besides, I put him in the ground, so my conscience is clear."

Grunting, Cartwright moved away, casting a glance over the dead Indians. "What about them?"

"We should burn them, but I'm mindful the smoke will give our position away. Both to the man who did the shooting here, and any friends of these poor bastards who might come looking for them."

"*Poor bastards*? I see nothing *poor* about these murdering heathens. But, if you think more savages will come, we'd best leave them here in the open to be picked at by the buzzards."

"Either way, others will come, alerted when this bunch don't return home to their camp, wherever that might be now. Whilst we're trying to catch up with the bank robbers, more Shoshone will be trying to catch up with us."

Cartwright blew out his cheeks and turned his gaze towards the direction they had come. "How long?"

"Soon. They'll be wondering why they haven't returned to camp and when they ride out and find the reason…" He shook his head. "It's a barrel of shit we've been placed in and someone just nailed down the lid."

"So maybe we should make a stand here."

"Against possibly twenty or thirty warriors? No, best if we try to make it to town, find out what the hell is going on. There's bound to be someone there who can tell us."

"And Deep Water?"

"He seems to have his own agenda. What the hell it is, beats me. He'll meet up with us, I have no doubt, but it'll be at a time of his choosing. So, let's saddle up and get as far away from this place as we can. We'll camp out under the stars, with no fire. You'll need a blanket."

"I thought Indians didn't attack at night?"

A slow smirk spread across Simms's face. "You've been listening to too many fairy-stories, boy. Indians fight at any time they choose, including at night. In fact, they relish it. You don't know they're close until they're pinning you down on the ground and slitting your throat."

The blood drained from Cartwright's face and he turned again to look out across the endless plain. "I wish to God I'd never set foot in this damnable place."

"Me too, boy. Me too."

Half a day's ride away, Sheriff Nathanial Mills stared across his desk at the big, bullish regulator standing before him. Either side were two deputies, their carbines trained on the big man, but Mills felt sure that if he wanted, Talpas could whip out those Navy Colts of his and finish every one of them off within the blink of an eye. The man's conceit gnawed away at him and the sooner he was out of town, the better Mills would feel.

"I should have insisted those two drifters over at the Silver Dime left town sooner than they did, but I had no just cause. Not until they took to beating the hell out of that other one. I'm not about to make the same mistake again."

Talpas shrugged and spread out his arms, as innocent as innocent can be. "But sheriff, I haven't given you any just cause either."

"You pulled a gun on Merve."

"Merve?"

"The barkeep at the saloon. You pulled a gun and you threatened him with it. We have witnesses."

"I needed information. I'll tell you what I told those others in the saloon – I'm on the trail of those drifters, as you call them. For your information, they're bank robbers, swindlers, cheats and liars and my task is to take them down." He smiled. "Any way I damn well please."

Mills felt his stomach pitch over and he thanked God he was sitting down. The man oozed danger and the Sheriff held no doubts such a man was capable of any number of dreadful acts, including cold-blooded killing. He was regulator after all, which was nothing more than a fancy word for an assassin. "Very well," Mills said, forcing the words out through a throat tight with anxiety, "you'd best be on your way."

"I sure will." The man's eyes drew away from the Sheriff's and settled on something on the wall behind him.

Frowning, Mills turned and squinted at the collection of wanted posters and announcements pinned there. When he turned again, Talpas' smile was now a grin. "You recognize someone on there? Another bounty maybe?"

Talpas put a finger to his forehead. "Just storing things away, Sheriff. I'm always open to new offers." He turned on his heels, and strode out.

The two deputies both released long, slow sighs of relief and Mills put his face in his hands and murmured, "Sweet Christ, that man scared the living hell out of me."

"Us two both," echoed one of the others. "Should we follow him, make sure he does as you told him?"

"No." Mills dropped his hands. "He has no reason to stay. It's the others he wants, thank God. No, we just try and gather up our wits again and go about living our lives as we did before all of this shit came down upon us."

"Until the next batch of no-gooders decides to pay us a call."

Something stirred inside Mills, something greater than any dread. An acceptance that one day, perhaps soon, an incident would occur that he wouldn't be able to contain. On the wrong side of fifty, time was hurtling towards his own, personal Day of Judgement. He didn't want to end his days with a bullet in his brain, so after the deputies trooped outside, he pulled out a slip of paper from his desk drawer and set to writing the letter he should have written years before. His resignation.

Fifteen

Painful progress across the plains

Simms leaned forward in his saddle and regarded the broken bridge for a long time, lost in thought. Cartwright scrambled around close by, muttering oaths more to himself than to anyone, kicking at stones, which caused tiny plumes of dust to rise. As this drifted across to Simms, the detective coughed, forcing the young lieutenant to stop and scowl. "This has been broken deliberately, Goddamnit!"

"Seems that way."

"What in the hell do we do now?"

"Go around, I guess. Find a way across."

"Where? What if there isn't one?"

"Bound to be. Somewhere."

"We could take it slow, lead the horses by hand, climb up the far side and—"

"It'll never happen. The horses will stumble, turn an ankle, maybe worse. Either way, we'd be stuck in the bottom with nowhere to go."

Cartwright exhaled loudly and launched a violent kick at the nearest stone, which proved not to be something small, but the tip of a much larger rock, its bulk buried in the ground. He yelped, hopping around as if scalded until he fell in the dirt, clutching at his boot. "God damn this country. And God damn you Simms! Time is running against us – if we lose that bastard, I'll hold you responsible."

"You need to calm down."

"Calm down? That murdering cur belongs at the end of a noose and if we all did what you do, we'd just mosey along in our own good time, with no sense of urgency. Well, to hell with that. I want him, Simms. I'm getting across this dried-up creek no matter what."

"Well, like I say, you'll have a hard time getting your horse across, but go right ahead. But don't come crying when she's lame and you're rolling around at the bottom with no horse to take you anywhere. Me, I'm heading down a ways, find a crossing place that won't kill me or my horse."

Cartwright glared, before turning his gaze to the pit of the crevice some twelve or so feet below him. "It ain't that far down."

"Must have been a reason someone put the bridge here. I'd be mighty careful if I were you." Turning his horse away, he eased his way off to the right, his pace slow and deliberate. He fully understood the young man's desire to confront Talpas. His need to find and kill the murderers of his father would be eating away at the young lieutenant like a cancer. The only way to stop it, to cut out its heart, was the fulfilment of his revenge. But recklessness wasn't going to do him any good and a twisted ankle, or worse, would combine with his shattered hand to render him a virtual invalid.

Within a few dozen paces, Cartwright came up alongside the Pinkerton. They rode in silence for a while, rounding an escarpment of bare rock before entering the open plain once again.

The minutes crept by. The dried creek meandered over to their left, both banks littered with broken rocks and jagged shale. "This is hopeless," said Cartwright, breaking the silence, his tone somewhat changed. Simms's wise words had tempered his impatience.

Declining to answer, Simms kept his face set straight ahead, picking out the details of the flat, bone-dry country, the occasional piece of scrub breaking up the otherwise uniform drabness.

They plodded along for well over an hour before Simms pulled on his reins and blew out a long sigh. Cartwright flashed him a sharp look. "You pissed? You pissed at making such a bad judgement? I'm pissed, but you wouldn't listen, would you? You had to—"

Simms held up his hand. "We got company."

Silence followed, Cartwright's demeanor again changing, but this time to one of open dread. He gulped down a swallow. "Company?"

Nodding, Simms slid down from his saddle and reached for his carbine. He drew it from its sheath and checked the load. "I'm not sure how many."

Cartwright squirmed around in his saddle, searching the horizon, the distant rocks, the bunches of gorse sprinkled here and there. "Where? I can't see anything."

"Straight ahead. There's an outcrop of rock yonder, with a small canopy of trees leading to a larger patch of woodland. Try not to stare, but it's clear to see."

He made no hint of any concern he may have had, going through the checking of his weapons with a careful, deliberate, almost mechanical action. Cartwright looked way off to the right, to the area Simms mentioned, but he could see nothing out of the ordinary, no movement, no shadows. Nothing. "Are you sure?"

"They swung around the rear of us some time ago, making off over that way to flank us. They were moving real slow, but I caught sight of 'em. They're on foot. They must have left their horses behind, maybe one of them taking them away in a much wider arc towards a patch of cover, hoping we wouldn't notice."

"Oh Jesus. They're Indians?"

"More than likely. And they'll be thinking we're the ones responsible for the killing of their friends."

"We have to tell them, for God's sake!"

Simms frowned. "Boy, they won't be up to having a friendly conversation with us. They'll kill us, after having stripped us naked, sliced off our balls, and pegging us out to dry."

Cartwright's bowels loosened, gut rumbling, and he released a powerful stench of wind, which caused Simms to wheel away. "I'm sorry," said Cartwright, voice trembling. "What the hell do we do?"

"We move in slow. Can you use that carbine of yours, with your bad hand and all?"

With his eyes wide with terror, Cartwright took some time to twist around and pull out his Colt Carbine, with its cylinder containing five rounds. "I use my arm as a rest. All I need is to find somewhere to lie down."

"Well, I'll see what I can do for you."

Ignoring the sarcasm, Cartwright straightened his back, making a brave show. "I can shoot real fine, Detective."

"Happy to hear it. I've also heard that gun of yours is prone to misfires, so best keep well away from me when you start shooting. Now listen, for this is what I propose we do. We continue nice and easy, you understand. We don't gallop or make as if we know they're there. But when I say 'break', you set your horse off to the right, keep your head down, and get to cover."

"And you, what will you do?"

"Why, shoot them, of course." And Simms winked.

For his part, all Cartwright could offer by way of a reply was to release another loud explosion of wind.

Sixteen

Cruel outcomes

Late afternoon, the hottest part of the day, but with the sun to his rear, Simms retained a clear view of the landscape before him. With confidence rising, he felt sure their pursuers would not be expecting such a reaction, but Simms had always believed taking the fight to the enemy was the best course. Slapping his horse's rump with the barrel of his carbine, he broke into a canter, glanced across to Cartwright, and hissed, "You ready?"

"Oh Jesus."

"Just keep your head down, boy. Get to cover, and shoot anything you see."

Cartwright licked lips dry from either the sun, or fear. Perhaps it was both.

"*Break!*" shouted Simms, and kicked his horse's flanks hard.

At the signal, Simms' voice so loud, Cartwright's horse bucked and wheeled away, spooked by the Pinkerton's sudden yell and burst into a gallop. Swearing, Cartwright fought to keep his animal under control, steering it to the right before allowing it to thunder off across the plain, nostrils snorting wildly.

Twisting around in his saddle, Simms couldn't help but grin as he watched the young lieutenant. He knew not how Cartwright would fair in the coming fight, but two guns were always better than one, even if one of them was inexperienced, frantic, and afraid. The odds were not in his favor, but they were all he had. Any odds against Indians were to be welcomed.

The first arrow sang overhead and he pressed himself down behind his horse's neck, making himself as low as possible. There was movement ahead, in the trees and he spotted the first buck looming out of the undergrowth, brown body blending in amongst the withered bracken, but enough for Simms to gauge the distance, to see the bow. Forty paces. The horse steamed forward, relentless, never veering from its course, even when the next arrow buzzed much closer than the first.

Ahead and slightly to the left, Simms spotted a spread of gorse, behind which several trees offered a semblance of cover. If he could make it before the arrows struck home, he'd be lucky, so he took the gamble, raised himself up and pulled hard on the reins. The horse screamed, snorting its annoyance and discomfort as the bit yanked back hard against its mouth. The animal's head came up, rear legs ploughing into the earth, a great cloud of dust and debris swirling around them both, and Simms took his chance and threw himself from the saddle. He hit the ground hard, his shoulder taking the full force of the impact, and he rolled in a tight ball, ignoring the pain. Ten years and more ago, he'd performed the same maneuver out on the battlefield, but his body was younger then, the results not quite the same as now. This time, the heavy impact jarred the carbine from his hands and it skidded way beyond reach. Angry, winded, and hurting, Simms scrambled towards the clump of parched vegetation, drawing the Navy Colt from his shoulder holster, firing two wild shots in the vague direction of his Indian assailant as another arrow singed through the air and thudded into a nearby tree.

Breathing hard, he fell in amongst the gorse, cursing loudly and tried to loosen his shoulder. He almost screamed at the pain. *Damn it to hell*, he cursed to himself, knowing his ill-thought action may lead to his undoing, for now useless limbs handicapped both him and the lieutenant. Any chance of an advantage was lost. He chanced a quick look across to the canopy of trees and cursed almost instantly.

The buck broke cover and charged, whooping at the top of his voice, crossing the short distance between his cover and where Simms lay, with terrifying swiftness. Despite the pain, Simms gritted his teeth and took steady aim with his revolver. Simms put two bullets into his assailant and grunted with grim satisfaction as the Indian cartwheeled over onto his side and lay quivering in the dirt.

With one more load in the chamber of the Navy, Simms knew there would be no time to put more powder and ball into the cylinder before the next attack. All told, with ten shots remaining, his plight was not so bad. His only concern was to how many more Shoshone braves lay hidden amongst the rocks and trees. He had the Dragoon, and the little Colt given to him by Pinkerton. The carbine he could see, lying there, but well beyond his reach. The dead Shoshone bore hatchet and knife, bow discarded, quiver empty, arrows spilled across the ground, so not much help there. Now the attack had begun, the dead Indian's companions may well wait him out. Within a few hours, night would fall. Death would soon follow.

Perhaps he should load up the Navy, he considered. But then, he saw movement ahead, and knew circumstances were turning against him. He could neither make a break for it, nor set up a fusillade. The only option was to wait. They had him trapped and his horse, strolling around some thirty feet or more away as if it were in a Chicago City park, offered no hope for retreat. He spat into the dirt, shifted position and stifled a cry as yet another stab of pain lanced through his upper arm. He took a few breaths whilst waiting for the discomfort to ease and tried to stretch out his limb. Instinctively, he ducked down as a booming blast from a Colt carbine resounded amongst the rocks over to his right. Grinning in grim satisfaction, Simms gave up a silent prayer of thanks. Cartwright was offering up the very type of covering fire which might deliver a chance for survival.

* * *

Dismounting behind the jagged, soaring and gleaming outcrop of rock rising many feet above him, Cartwright paused, battling to calm his pounding heart. He wiped the sweat from his brow, his legs quivered as if the muscles were jelly, and his stomach rolled and rumbled. Not certain what to do, or which direction to take, he waited in a crouch, senses straining, hoping none of the Indians had noticed his approach.

The sound of a screaming horse forced him to jerk himself upright. Mouth hanging open, throat dry, he positioned the barrel of the carbine across the forearm of his redundant arm and eased back the hammer, engaging the first round of the full cylinder. Shots rang out ahead of him. A revolver. So, not Indians, perhaps Simms. The attack had begun, and now he must do his part.

Swallowing down his fear, he eased himself between the rocks, which formed a kind of barrier between himself and the open ground, and slithered over their smooth, baking hot surface. Forcing himself to stay low, his concentration centered on any movements or sounds. Two more shots cut through the hot air and he almost yelped in surprise. He stopped, half expecting a screaming group of savages to descend upon him, hatchets raised, murder in their hearts.

But no attack came.

Settling himself again for a few moments, he dropped in between the cracks of a group of larger boulders, and continued his steady approach around the foot of the great, looming rock.

The first knowledge Cartwright had of the buck was when the Indian landed solidly in the small of his back, projecting him into the ground, breath expelled with a loud gush. Shock and the impact combined to cause his finger to squeeze on the trigger, the carbine blasting with a huge boom, the noise amplified by the encroaching rocks.

Something yanked his head backwards, the hair on his scalp wrenched almost from the roots. He squawked, knowing his life had reached its end. Within a blink, the knife would slice through the ligaments and arteries of his neck, the pain intense, but thankfully brief. At least, this was his hope. He offered up a frantic, garbled prayer, his thoughts everywhere – panic, dread, and despair, mixing together to cloud his judgement.

He waited, knowing it should be over. Longing for it to be over.

Instead, the grip on his hair lessened, and then, unbelievably, he was free. He rolled over, unsure what he would see. The malicious grin, the teeth exposed, knife preparing to deliver the final blow…

The Indian stared, eyes glazing over with something akin to disbelief. He dropped to his knees, words rattling in his throat, and toppled over to his side.

Gaping, Cartwright dared not believe what he saw. Was he already dead? A shadow fell over him and he looked up, confused, but relieved beyond measure.

Deep Water stood looking across to the other outcrops of rock, alert, ignoring the unspoken questions flitting across Cartwright's bewildered face. The knife in the scout's hand dripped blood. He stooped, wiped the blade on the dead buck's pants, and motioned towards the canopy of trees on the other side of the rocks. "How many?"

Cartwright shook his head, unable to unscramble his mind and find any words, still coming to terms with the fact he was alive.

Ignoring him, Deep Water melted into the surroundings, leaving the young lieutenant to sit stunned, waiting until he found the strength, and the courage, to follow.

Simms bit down on his bottom lip, swallowing down the cry of pain as he tried to stretch out his arm. He sank back, sucking in breath, cursing his luck and his stupidity. The shoulder was dislocated, he knew it. Better than being broken, he mused, but being incapacitated this way, if any of the Shoshone closed in on him he wouldn't stand a chance.

Grunting, he got to his knees, risking another arrow, but none came. He wondered about that for a moment. Almost all the warriors would be armed with bows, of that he was certain. This had to be a ploy, to lure him out from behind his cover. They had no way of knowing how many guns he had, and they'd witnessed their companion fall so they were aware of their quarry's skill in killing, making them cautious. Nevertheless, he couldn't remain here for long. With night closing in, the odds would be with the Indians. The distance between him and the canopy of trees was something like thirty or so paces. He might make it, he might not, but choices no longer remained. As soon as the sun dropped down below the horizon, he would make a break for it, hit them before they hit him. So with his mind made up, he dipped behind his sparse cover once more and waited.

* * *

Deep Water moved with a stealth borne out of years of living off the land, stalking game, moving as if invisible. He took the first warrior in the back, the knife penetrating deep, slicing through internal organs, and before the man dropped dead to the ground, Deep Water moved on, low, silent, alert.

He came upon two more, nocked arrows waiting. They turned to see him and rose, readying themselves, but he was too swift, the blade slashing across the first's throat, sweeping around to sink into the second's gut. So close, they stared into one another's eyes. The Shoshone tried to speak, but managed only a grunt as Deep Water buried the knife deeper still. The warrior hung onto him, a desperate embrace, a silent plea to allow him to live. Gritting his teeth, Deep Water pushed and the Shoshone went limp and slid from the blade, lifeless.

The first warrior was writhing amongst the bracken, clutching at his throat. The strike had been clean, but not penetrating, so Deep Water finished him, stabbing hard into the throat of the stricken warrior and kept the knife there until all of the fight left the man and he too died.

Reaching down, he picked up one of the bows, fitted an arrow and stuck several more into his belt. The knife he sheathed before moving on.

A slight breeze rustled through the leaves. Here, amongst the trees, the air was cool, the atmosphere almost tranquil. He drank water from his canteen and listened. Nothing stirred and he rested, knowing his task was not yet complete. Somewhere in this glade other Shoshone warriors waited, hidden, out for revenge and they wouldn't stop until they achieved success. He closed his eyes, clearing his mind of what he'd done so far, for he knew he still had much to do.

Spotting a movement amongst the trees, he killed the next warrior with a well-aimed arrow, the point hitting the warrior in the temple and travelling through into the brain. When yet another broke cover and rose from behind a nearby tree, Deep Water shot him in the chest. The Shoshone stumbled backwards, clawing at overhanging branches, desperate to remain on his feet. But as he struggled to stay alive, Deep Water was on him, the knife flashing through the air, and it was over.

In the space of a few violent minutes, how many warriors had he killed? Not wanting to count, Deep Water fell down with the tree at his back and stared into the distance, his mouth slack, body numb with shock. No longer able to keep the images from invading his thoughts, the enormity of it all brought a bout of violent trembling to his body. He took to rocking himself, knees crunched up to his chest, arms wrapped around them and as he rocked, the tears rolled down his face and he grew blind to his surroundings.

Cartwright slipped, cracking his knee against a piece of coarse rock, and he swore, rubbing the abrasion vigorously. He sat down on the offending rock and wished he'd brought his water canteen. But, like the fool he was, he'd left it with his horse, the animal hobbled on the far side of the large rock.

Cursing, he climbed to his feet and winced, moved his knee backwards and forwards in a swinging motion to ease the pain. The movement helped, and satisfied, he crept on, albeit more gingerly this time.

A blur of movement ahead and slightly to his left, forced him to stop and he crouched, readying his carbine, the barrel across his right forearm, left thumb easing back the hammer. With a great explosion of breaking branches and trampled undergrowth, a Shoshone came crashing through the trees, tomahawk raised. But not towards him. The warrior pounded across his line of sight and Cartwright quickly got to his feet, pain ignored, and moved over the outcrops of rock in pursuit.

With only one useable arm, the carbine grew unwieldy, so he lay it down against a nearby rock, and pulled out the Navy Colt from his hip holster. At a half run, he moved across the rocks, eyes fixed ahead and heard the whooping of the Indian attacker. There were other sounds too, of undergrowth breaking, of thrashing, grunting, cries of desperation. He pushed on, the pain in his knee forgotten, and moved deeper into the surrounding glade.

He came upon them within a few paces. Two Indians, locked in a desperate hand-to-hand fight. The Shoshone had Deep Water pinned, with one hand gripping his throat, the other holding the tomahawk, raised to strike. But Deep Water had the man's wrist, and both strained, faces distorted with the effort, eyes bulging, flesh red and growing redder.

Cartwright levelled his revolver. He was three paces away, and the shot was an easy one.

He hesitated.

There was something about the scout. He carried a secret. His surly manner, his dismissive arrogance and contempt, almost as if he was using both white men for his own purpose. But what purpose? He'd watched Deep Water talk to the dying man earlier before riding off at a great pace. To where? For what? Had the man, mortally wounded by the long-hair, told him some vital secret? And if so, why hadn't the scout shared it?

A loud, high-pitched squeal brought him out of his reverie. The Shoshone, his fist cracking for a second time across his victim's jaw, had the upper hand now. He lifted Deep Water to his feet and slammed his knee into Deep Water's groin. The scout howled, clutching himself, and dropped to his knees, doubled-up, the fight over. The Shoshone, his naked body dripping with sweat, threw back his head and let out a wild, prolonged whoop of victory.

Cartwright raised the Navy Colt and shot the Shoshone warrior three times in the back, each bullet blowing him forward before he landed and lay still amongst the undergrowth. No other movement or sound followed, the silence eerie after such a sudden eruption of violence. Glancing down, the lieutenant looked at his hand and saw it was shaking, so he sat on the closest rock and wished he too were dead.

From out of the corner of his eyes, he became aware of Deep Water standing, breathing hard and taking a few tentative steps before sitting on another rock directly opposite the young lieutenant.

For how long they both sat, neither knew, and nothing passed between them. No questions, no comments. If Deep Water was aware of Cartwright's hesitation in killing his Shoshone assailant, he made no mention, merely stared at the ground.

Until another warrior appeared.

Deep Water reacted first, grabbing wildly for the bow. Cartwright, reacting too slowly, only had time to swivel and look across to the closest cluster of rocks and the man standing there, feet planted firmly on the rocks, Cartwright's carbine in his hands.

The seconds crawled by. The warrior had a maniacal look about him, teeth gritted white in his teak-colored face, his body rippling with muscles, eye trained down the length of the barrel as he took careful aim.

Cartwright closed his eyes, not knowing if the bullet would strike him first, or Deep Water. He cared not. He'd had enough of killing, of riding, of thoughts of vengeance eating through his morality. So he waited, in silent acceptance of his fate.

When the carbine boomed, he tensed in preparation for the lead shot to smack into his body. It didn't. Deep Water was the preferred target then. He snapped open his eyes, looked, and saw Deep Water standing unharmed, the bow half-drawn, his face aghast, staring in disbelief.

Turning his head to confront the Shoshone, Cartwright blinked with incomprehension towards the open space. The warrior was no longer there. Confused, the lieutenant got to his feet, the Navy Colt heavy in his hand, and moved over to where the warrior had stood. He took his time, fighting to control the shaking of his gun hand. What mad, insane trick could this be?

On reaching the rock, he realized there never was any kind of trick. The warrior lay on his back, half his face nothing but a mangled, bloody mess, blown away. The carbine lay close by, smoking and shattered. The weapon had misfired, as Simms said it was prone to do. And the result had proved catastrophic.

Cartwright collapsed on the ground, not knowing whether to cry out with joy or despair. All he knew was that it was over.

For now.

Seventeen

Revelations in the town of Burybridge

After Cartwright stepped out from amongst the trees and called across to Simms, they made camp as the sun set. Deep Water examined Simms shoulder, told him to brace himself, and wrenched the joint back into its socket with an audible snap. Simms screeched in pain, flinging himself backwards, gritting his teeth. Gradually his face relaxed, anguish replaced with utter, joyous relief. He sat up and smiled his thanks as Deep Water wrapped a firm dressing, fashioned from strips torn from an old shirt, around the detective's damaged shoulder to help with recovery.

Melancholy descended over them all. No-one wanted to eat, drink or sleep. At some point, with dusk turning to night, Deep Water wandered amongst the trees. Cartwright watched the scout go, then turned to Simms. "Something's changed in him."

"Killing does that."

Nodding, Cartwright picked up a nearby twig and started to scratch random designs in the dirt. "There was a point when I sort of gave up. When that Shoshone was about to kill me with my own gun… I took stock. I don't think I can do this any longer, Detective."

"Give it time. We all need to find our own way to come to terms with what we do, but you made your decision to ride with me to find justice for your father. Killing Indians wasn't part of that, but circumstance played against us all. In the morning, we can readjust, set our minds once more on what we have to do."

"Readjust? Jesus, you think I can do that after what happened here today?" he spat, raising the stick and hurling it away as anger overtook him. "I wanted so much to watch that Indian kill Deep Water, you know that? I stood and I watched and I did nothing. Not until it was almost over, then I shot him. In the back. What does that make me, Detective?" Simms stared back, no answer given. Cartwright cackled with disgust. "I'll tell you – a murdering sonofabitch, that's what it makes me."

"No, it doesn't. That Indian would have killed Deep Water, then turned around and done the same to you. You saved the scout's life."

"But I *hesitated*. Why in the name of God would I do that?"

"I don't know. You tell me."

Rubbing his face, Cartwright appeared to be inwardly struggling with himself, uncertain as to whether to reveal his fears.

"Listen," said Simms, hoping to encourage the young officer to be forthcoming, "I've had doubts too."

"Doubts? What sort of doubts?"

"About his reasons for being with us."

"But you kept them to yourself?"

"Only because I wasn't totally sure, but… Why not tell me what's eating you, Lieutenant?"

"Very well, I'll try. When I rode off and left you, to find those murdering bastards out on the prairie, I saw the way the sharpshooter killed the Indians, and I'm ashamed to say it, I was so damned afraid I couldn't move. I saw him step up to the other one, and they spoke for a few moments and then the sharpshooter, for I knew it was him with his buckskins and his long flowing hair, I saw him shoot the other guy in the guts. I squatted down amongst the rocks and I prayed to Jesus to help me stay hidden. And all the while, I was crying. Crying like a little baby. I heard a horse, so I chanced a look to see the sharpshooter riding off. But even then, I didn't have the courage to move. I just sat, shaking, and I could hear the other one crying out in agony. When Deep Water rode up, he got down and talked to him. I don't know what was said, but then he took off also, in the direction of the sharpshooter."

"You're thinking our scout has some sort of personal vendetta going on?"

"He might have; I don't know, but I don't trust him, I'm sure of that. Better he was dead than have him slit our throats in the night."

"He won't do that."

"How do you know?"

Simms shrugged, but the action brought a stab of pain from his still-damaged shoulder, and he reached across and massaged the offending joint with his other hand. "If he'd wanted to, he would have done so already. And he came back, didn't he? Saved both of us from almost certain death."

"I know." Cartwright turned away, pressing a finger and thumb into his eyes. "Jesus, I *know*."

"But that's not to say I'm in disagreement with you. He acts mighty strange at times, almost as if he has his mind on something else. I reckon he has some sort of grudge."

"With the sharpshooter?"

"Could be. He didn't finish off the other one, did he? Left him to bleed to death."

"Maybe he thought that was a greater punishment?"

"Maybe. Or maybe that fella had nothing to do with causing Deep Water harm – whatever that harm might be."

Cartwright blew out a loud breath. "I'm just so sick, sick of it all. Being out here, the Indians, the killing. I don't..." He sniffed loudly, dropped his hand and blew out a loud breath. "I don't want to do this anymore. Regardless of what you said, Detective, I'm just not cut out for this sort of thing. I'm sorry."

For a long time, neither spoke. Eventually, Simms stretched himself out on the ground, and drew his blanket across himself. No sooner had he done so, than Deep Water returned. He squatted down beside the fire, poking around at the embers with a stick. "I found their ponies. The last one, the one that killed himself with the lieutenant's rifle, he must have brought them. There are no other signs. All of them are dead."

Throughout the remainder of the night, they took turns taking watch in case any more Shoshones came charging out of the darkness. None did, proving the truth of Deep Water's words. In the morning, Simms rolled his shoulders and didn't experience even a twinge. Together, the three men dragged the corpses into a grotesque pile and burnt them. No one spoke as the flames lapped around the bodies, fat crackling, flesh burning. Afterwards, Cartwright brewed up coffee and Simms marveled at how well the young man acquitted himself, having the use of a single hand.

"We going to continue along the creek, find a way across?" asked Cartwright, blowing across the top of his steaming tin cup.

Simms nodded and was about to speak, when Deep Water, not drinking himself, interjected. "I have found a way, to the town."

The others looked at him, but he said nothing more. Packing up their horses, they set out across the plain with the scout leading. Again, he proved as good as his word. Within an hour, the creek was sufficiently shallow enough for them to take the horses across without danger of falling. On the far side, they broke into a canter and headed for the town of Burybridge.

Their first stop was a merchant store, where they bought supplies. Cartwright browsed amongst the various items for sale whilst Simms bartered over the price of corn and ammunition. The lieutenant came across a number of ancient muskets stacked in the corner and amongst them, an eighteen-fifty-one pattern Sharps carbine, which he showed Simms over at the counter.

"That's as good as new," said the storekeeper, sucking at his teeth, but before he could continue, Simms put two silver dollars in front of him. The man tilted his head, thought for a moment, then grinned. "Hot diggity," he said, sweeping up the money, "that'll do just fine, mister."

Stepping outside, they paused to allow their eyes to readjust to the sunlight. Cartwright was admiring his new gun, but Simms was staring down the street. He had a box of cartridges under his arm, while in his hands he bore two large bags of grain for the horses. It was difficult to know what he might do, but he knew he had to do something. For below them was Deep Water, and there were two other men on either side of him with rifles trained at his head. A third, sporting a large, dull-metal sheriff's badge, was in the act of readjusting a pair of handcuffs around the scout's wrists.

"You mind telling me what the hell you think you're doing?"

The sheriff paused and turned to face Simms, one eyebrow arched. "What did you say?"

"I asked you what the hell you think you're doing to my scout."

"*Your* scout? Well, that's mighty interesting, I must say," the sheriff snarled before clicking the handcuffs shut. He turned and faced Simms square on, both hands on his hips, the butt of his revolver clearly visible in the holster at his hip. "And who in the name of God Almighty might you be?"

"I'm Detective Simms, of the Pinkerton Detective Agency, and I'm on the trail of train robbers. That man is my scout and you have no right to restrain him the way you have."

"Well now, *Mister* Pinkerton detective, let me tell you something. This is my town and we have a fine community here. We don't take kindly to allowing savages to wander amongst our townsfolk. Town ordnances state quite clearly, all such lowlifes and non-persons should be detained whilst awaiting trial by our very own Judge Cyrus James. He is a man, as I'm sure you well know, who is held in the highest esteem, well qualified in law and—"

"I couldn't give a good damn who he is, or what your reasons are for treating Deep Water in this way, but I'll tell you this – you either let him go, or I'll do so myself."

One of the deputies guffawed, "Tough talk when we have two guns on your friend here. What you aiming to do, mister? Bore us all to death?"

His friend joined in, head bobbing as he laughed, "Pinkerton Detective my ass. What the hell is that anyway? Something out of a theatre show back East?"

"Bordello more like!"

They both roared at this.

"Shut the fuck up," spat the sheriff, his narrowed eyes never leaving the detective. The two deputies immediately stopped their inane laughter and the air grew chill. "He will remain in the town jail until such time as I can fetch Judge James. Until then, I'll be asking you to hand over your firearms."

"For what cause?" said Cartwright, moving his weight from one foot to the other.

The sheriff didn't blink. "Because I say so."

Simms pursed his lips. "You'll have to allow me to put down this grain first."

"Do it," said the sheriff, his hand creeping towards his own gun. "Nice and slow."

Complying, Simms leaned forward slightly and placed the two bags on the boardwalk, with the box of cartridges on top. He straightened himself up and pulled back his coat. "I have two handguns."

"Lay them both on the floor, then kick them away. Your friend here can place that carbine at his feet."

A nod, a smile. Nothing to give any hint as to what was about to occur. In a blur, the Navy materialized in Simms hand, the Dragoon in the other and the first shot blew off the sheriff's hat. As the man staggered backwards, mouth working furiously, Simms put a shot at the feet of the first deputy, came down the steps to street level and rammed the muzzle of the big firearm into the sheriff's forehead.

"You sorry bastard," squealed the sheriff, all of his former bravado lost to the wind, "you could have killed me!"

"If I'd meant to kill you, you'd already be dead. Now," he nodded over to the two deputies, both standing transfixed, blood drained from their faces, "you release my friend and we'll be on our way."

"Ask him where the big man went," said Cartwright, coming down to join the Pinkerton. He was struggling to control his breathing. "You mealy-mouthed son-of-a-whore, answer the question or I shall kill you myself," and to give emphasis to his words, he prodded the sheriff hard in the gut with the point of the carbine. "Which way did he go?"

"I don't know who you're talking about."

"Yes you do," said Simms evenly. "We know he came here, Deep Water followed his tracks. Now, you tell us, or I'll allow my friend here to put a hole as big as a canyon in your belly."

The sheriff fell to his knees, hands raised, a frantic, terrified look etched into every line of his face. "Oh, sweet Jesus, don't kill me."

Cartwright snarled and eased back the hammer of his gun.

One of the deputies, deciding the time for bravery was past, stepped forward, "I'll tell you. His name was Talpas. He came here looking for his buddies, but they'd rode off some time before. Four of them."

"Release my friend," said Simms.

Without a pause, the deputy reached towards Deep Water, fitted a tiny key into the cuffs, and released him. Deep Water, rubbing his wrists, swept up the man's rifle, then tore the other from the second deputy's grip.

"So, that was his name," continued Simms. "Talpas. Beaudelaire Talpas."

"You know him?"

"Heard of him, but never met him. A regulator, so I believe, employed by some of the local mining companies to shoot any hostiles who may stray too close. Red or White. His reputation somewhat precedes him."

"Well, this Talpas, he was mighty insistent, as you are too, to know what became of those others. He was not a man to face off with, if you get my meaning. The sheriff here told him where his friends went and he left."

"And where did they go."

"They headed for Fort Bridger, although I do believe they were preparing to have a rendezvous some miles from there."

"You're mighty obliging," said Simms holstering the Dragoon, but keeping the Navy in his grip. "If I find you've lied to me, I'll come back, and I'll kill you. You know that."

"Yes I do, and I ain't lying. I swear it."

"You heap of pigswill, Sommers," piped up the sheriff, still on his knees. "I'll bust your sorry ass for this."

Grinning, Simms looked down at the lawman. "You're a hard-sounding old bastard, but not such a clear thinking one. Why did you tell Talpas what he wanted to know?"

"It's like Sommers said – he was mean, that Talpas. Meaner than any man I've ever come across. He had dead eyes, a killer's eyes."

"And you know about such things?"

"I served in the Mexican War. I've seen death many times, and those that perpetrated such things."

Simms pressed his lips together. "Well, I served too, so I have an awareness of what you're saying. It is your opinion this Talpas was in the War also?"

"Could be. He certainly carried himself that way. A man of violence. I didn't want to cross such a man."

"And yet you served."

"I was with munitions, driving supply wagons. I never saw action."

"Well, you don't need to do soldiering in order to perform your duty."

"But you did. Saw action, I mean. I recognize it."

Grunting, Simms looked towards the deputies. "Sommers, you pick up my grain and then we'll head over to the jail. You can while away a few hours inside whilst my companions and I take our leave."

"I'll hunt you down for this," said the sheriff.

"Well, that's your prerogative, but know this. A lot of things can go wrong out on the range. Snakes, mountain lions, Indians… You could be lying out there for years, shot dead, and no one would ever find you." Simms winked. "My advice would be to stay at home, put your feet up, take it easy. No point in putting yourself and everyone you know in danger."

The sheriff swallowed hard. "Those things could befall you, just as easily."

"Yes they could, but you see, I already have an Indian, and my friend here, he's as strong as a lion… As for the snake, well," he motioned with the Navy, "I'm a might quicker than any rattler, sheriff. A darn sight deadlier too." He holstered his gun, reached down, and picked the sheriff up by the shirtfront, whilst deftly relieving him of the handgun at his side.

Deep Water banged the jail door closed and turned the key. He crossed the room to where Simms and Cartwright stood, and put the bunch of keys on the sheriff's desk.

Simms nodded his thanks, then motioned towards the wall and the collection of posters pinned there. One in particular took his interest and he moved around the desk and stared at it more keenly. "I'll be damned," he said and took it down. As he read it, he went over to the jail and held the poster up so the sheriff could see it. "When did this come in?"

The sheriff shrugged. "Weeks ago. I'm not sure."

"This man," said Simms, flicking at the paper with the back of his fingers, "he was found buried in a shallow grave, it says."

"With his identity papers. It's posted in most of the towns here in the Territory. Circuit judge wanted to try and get more particulars, find out if anyone knew him. Maybe you do?"

"I know *of* him, by name only, but had no idea what he looked like. I was kind of hoping this was the man I was looking for."

"Well, if he was, you've found him. Dead as a post. Those that found him think he was bushwhacked before his killer threw him in the ditch."

"Why were they looking for him?"

"He was seen with another guy, but after they left together, neither was seen again. Apparently, he left owing some money – quite a sizeable sum so I understand. Either ways, he was found, only partially buried. Listen," the sheriff stepped up close to the bars, gripping them, "if you are a Detective, then perhaps you should investigate it. In the meantime, how in the hell are you proposing we should get out this jail, with the keys being all the way across the room?"

"I'll leave a note. On the door." Simms folded up the poster, tipped his hat and went outside. Cartwright and Deep Water followed, the Indian closing the outside door behind him.

"You look concerned, Detective."

Simms looked keenly at Cartwright and sighed. "I am. The man on the poster, he was the one I was certain was with the gang who robbed the train. The sharpshooter."

"So, if it wasn't him, then it has to be Talpas."

"Yes, seems that way. And yet…" Shaking his head, Simms strode across the street, mind filled with confusion. Whoever this Talpas was, he seemed to have materialized out of thin air. For a man to shoot as well as he did, he thought old sergeant Brewer would know of him. But the only person he mentioned was Ishmael Farage, and now, as the poster showed – he was dead.

Eighteen

Railroad camp, south of Fort Bridger

On the rise, the three men reined in their horses and gazed down into the valley stretching out before them. In the center lay the sprawl of the worker's camp. Simms readjusted himself in his saddle, his backside sore after such a long ride, and directed his gaze towards Deep Water. "I'm thinking it might be wise if you were to stay here, away from this hellish place. Sorry to have to say it, but there will be many there who hate your kind, having suffered themselves or heard stories from others."

Giving no answer, Deep Water merely watched, face blank.

"As soon as we've picked up some news, we'll ride back to you."

"The trail might continue. I will look further east."

"But we'll lose you," said Cartwright and for a moment he appeared awkward, looking away, not wishing the scout to catch his eye. "We need you, Deep Water."

"Best stay here," insisted Simms. "I don't know what your interest is in these men, and I don't wish to press you on it, but the way you are makes me believe you have your own agenda."

"It is the same as yours."

"I hope so, Deep Water."

"They did something to you," said Cartwright, continuing to look in the other direction. "I don't know what, but I've noticed your look."

Sighing, Deep Water turned his pony away. "I shall make camp close by."

"Then you'll tell us."

The scout arched a single eyebrow as Cartwright's face at last turned to him. The young lieutenant didn't avert his gaze this time, his stare hard, unflinching. "There is nothing much to tell."

"I think maybe there is."

Another sigh and Deep Water dropped his gaze and wheeled his horse away, heading towards a small depression amongst the broken ground.

Not wishing to pursue his thoughts further, Simms led his horse carefully down the other side of the escarpment. Cartwright followed.

"You think he'll stay up there?"

Simms shrugged. "I reckon he'll do whatever he needs to do."

"But if he goes chasing after them, we'll have no chance of finding their trail."

"Let's hope he waits, then."

"You seem mighty unconcerned, Detective. What if he goes off and—"

"He can 'go off' any time he pleases, Lieutenant. In the dead of night if he so chooses. There's not a great deal either you nor I can do about it. All we can hope for is that he stays right where he is until we learn something."

"You think he has his own agenda then, just like you said?"

"There's something, yes. For sure. Maybe someone in the gang wronged him, or stole something. I don't know, but if he goes off riding across the open plain and Talpas spots him, he's dead. That man is a dead-eye shot, Lieutenant. That's something we all need to be aware of."

Both men fell into silence as they set off, the only sound the steady clump of horse hooves upon the baked earth. Within half an hour, they reached the outskirts of the camp.

They walked into the eclectic mix of broken down shacks, tents and half-constructed boarding houses and saloons with the clouds gathering on the horizon like a precursor to some dread event. Men mingled in small groups, clothes grey with dust, faces etched with toil, grim and gleaming with sweat. These were railroad workers, hard lives hewn by the pick and the shovel, endless days of heaping ballast, laying sleepers and rails, backs and shoulders screaming with the effort. Tough men, from every corner of the globe, many of them drinking, some laughing, most so tired they could barely stand. Thunder rumbled but no one stirred. If it rained, their labor might slow, but it wouldn't stop. The railroad company looked to only profit, and they would allow nothing to stand in its way.

Aware of the many eyes following them, when they stopped in front of a clapped-out hotel, Simms twisted in his saddle and grunted. "We'd best take care here, Lieutenant. Let me ask the questions."

"And if we don't learn anything?"

"Then we leave, without a single backward glance. You understand me? Some of these boys are hard-boiled mean and will slit your throat if you give them so much as a sideways glance. So, stay close, and don't make no hasty moves towards your gun."

"How you gonna play it?"

"You'll see."

And Simms slid down from his horse, waited for Cartwright to follow, then stepped up towards the doors of the saloon and went inside.

It stank of stale beer and sweat, mingled amidst the heavy fog of tobacco smoke. Despite the afternoon not yet drifting into evening, workers of every size, race and age filled the place with their stinking bodies. Conversation and laughter mingled with the slapping of cards onto tables and the slam of empty glasses on the bar counter.

Everything ceased when Simms came through the door.

Pulling up behind the lawman, Cartwright breathed, "Shit," but said nothing more.

Questioning, suspicious glares glowered from every face, but Simms ignored them and crossed to the counter. Two men worked behind it, as both alike as twins, dressed in neat black waistcoats, white shirts decorated with bootlace ties, hair short-cropped. One, whose only discernible difference to his colleague was a thin pencil moustache, stepped away from the large gilt-framed mirror behind him, planted both hands flat on the counter top, and said, "Gentleman."

Nodding, Simms leaned side on against the bar whilst scanning the room, holding the occasional pair of eyes, searching the faces. "Two whiskies," he said.

"I have bourbon or Scotch."

"I'm impressed. One of each."

Without a word, the barman produced two, small glasses and filled them up with the request. "Two bits, sir."

Simms placed a dollar coin on the counter top and pushed it across. "For some more later."

Taking up one of the glasses, Simms breathed in the aroma, grunted his satisfaction, and raised the bourbon towards the assembled band of workers, none of whom had yet moved or spoken. "Your good health, gentlemen," and then he downed it in one.

A few answered his toast in muffled tones, most didn't, choosing to turn away and return to whatever they were doing. Slowly, conversations returned, the humor now dulled; suspicion however, lingered in every sideways glance.

"That's a fine blend," said Simms, returning the empty glass to the counter.

"We receive batches from New Orleans," explained the barman, taking the glass and putting it out of sight.

"That's a fair way."

"You been there? I hear it's a wondrous place."

"I have, some years back. I rode across from Texas… not a journey I'd like to repeat in a hurry."

"Well, perhaps you won't need to. The railroad is opening up the Territory more and more with every passing day. These gentlemen you see around you are the force behind its success."

As Cartwright moved up alongside him, Simms slid the second glass across. "Sample that, Lieutenant."

Simms caught the shooting glance from the second barman, at his place next to the mirror. "Are you Army men, sir?"

"We were. We are now… How can I put it…"

"Regulators?" The second barman shuffled closer, cleaning a glass with perhaps too much force. When it cracked and shattered beneath his bar-towel, he cursed, but made no move to clear it up.

"The railroad company has employed us to help protect its workers," said Simms, and as his words drifted amongst the men, the conversations again grew quiet, games of poker and chance pausing for a moment. "Shoshone warbands are circling as we speak."

"Shoshone?"

A big individual climbed up out of his chair and stepped forward. He wore heavy-duty overalls, a sweat-stained shirt underneath, with an ancient, tattered Derby hat pushed back on his head. From out the top of his waistband projected the butt of a revolver – old, and by the way the metal was pitted and spotted, not often used.

"That's right," continued Simms as the man drew nearer, lifting his eyes from the gun to take in the full size of the man. He was a giant, hands like plates, and

Simms craned his neck to keep his eyes fixed on the man's florid, concerned face. "Have you noticed any whilst working?"

"None at all. But there was a man here, who said much the same thing."

"Ah," Simms nodded, as if in understanding, and gave a nod to the barman. "I'll take those other whiskies now, if I may." He smiled and looked at the huge bear of a man once more. "Big fella, long hair? Wearing buckskin clothes with a rifle almost as tall as you?"

"That's him."

"His name's Talpas. Beaudelaire Talpas. He may have been riding with some other fellas."

"He said he was *looking* for some others, but we've seen no other strangers drifting through."

"Let me buy you a drink," said Simms, motioning to the barman. "Whisky?"

"I don't drink with hired killers."

Simms held his breath and turned to face the giant. "Call me a protector, if you have a mind to. I'm not here to kill any workers, friend."

"I'm not your friend, and as for being protected, you think I need protecting?"

The silence closed in, the atmosphere charged, expectant. Even the barmen halted their tasks. A few of the workers put down their drinks and left the saloon. Simms watched them go before he turned again to the big man. "Shoshone warriors could come in here in the dead of night and slit your throat before you even knew it. I know. I've been hunting and killing them for the past ten years."

"Is that a fact?"

"Yes, it is. And they're on the warpath. No one is safe, not even someone as big and as capable as you."

"We've heard nothing about the hiring of regulators," said the barman with the moustache. "We've heard stories about them operating up in the old goldmines, but not here, not on the railroad."

"The deeper into the Territory the railroad goes, the more likely it is you'll encounter Indians. They won't greet you with a hearty smile, you can count on that."

The giant gave a short, scoffing laugh. "The other one, the one you described, he said nothing about no warbands coming close, only that he was hired to kill 'em. He said he needed to talk to those others, that they had important information. You a friend of his?"

"Not exactly, no."

"What then?"

Simms shrugged. "Did he happen to say which direction he was taking?"

"You seem mighty interested in him, mister. If not a friend, what is he to you?"

"Colleague."

"I thought as much. Talpas, you said?"

"Beaudelaire Talpas, yes."

"Coulson," said the barman, wringing his hands, growing edgy, "you go back to your friends now. I'm sure our visitor here will take his—"

"He came here yesterday, asking about his friends. He'd been down to the 'Lucky Strike' saloon before he visited us all in here." The man called Coulson leaned forward, using his enormous frame as a means to intimidate – an action which no doubt, had worked many times before, but had little effect on Simms, who remained disinterested. Coulson, feathers ruffled, jabbed a single meaty finger into Simms chest. "Whatever he is, this *friend* of yours, you give him a message."

"I told you. I know him, but he ain't no friend. A colleague is all, like I said."

Something in the way Simms spoke sent a wave of uncertainty, perhaps even disbelief, across the room. A few more men left the bar, and others stood, backing away, fidgeting, murmuring. Standing not two paces away, Cartwright drummed his fingers on the bar.

Coulson sneered. "He spoke to one or two of *my* friends, this Talpas, but not in no polite fashion, if you get my meaning."

"Perhaps you should expand."

"*Expand?* I'll tell you what I'll do, regulator piece of shit, I'll send you over to him in a box. He shot my friends, that's what he did, both of 'em. In the knees. They'll not work again, not for no railroad, not for anyone." Another jab of the finger. "He may as well just have killed them, poor bastards."

"Coulson," said the barman again, almost coming across the counter, "I want no trouble here. If you start anything, Mr. Fergusson will fire your fat ass."

"Stick it up yours, Toby. This here regulator is just the same. Ain't you, piece of regulator shit?"

"I told you, he ain't no friend. I know what he can do, so nothing you've said so far surprises me, but I ain't like him." Simms smiled. "Unless pushed."

"Is that supposed to unsettle me? Because if it is, you has failed."

In a blur, the big man's fist went back, but what followed came faster and a good deal more furious. The swinging punch struck nothing but thin air. If it had connected, nobody could doubt Simms would be dead. But it didn't connect. Simms ducked, slipping the blow, and drove his own left fist hard into the big man's solar plexus, knocking the wind out of him. With a great bellow, Coulson folded and Simms, whipping out the Dragoon, swung it around in a tight arc and cracked it into the big man's temple, felling him to his knees, stunned.

The heavy, metallic, double-click of the hammer being cocked froze everyone in the room solid. Simms put the tip of the barrel against Coulson's head. The Pinkerton had barely broken a sweat. "I'll kill you, big fella, right here, right now. Cartwright, relieve this gentleman of his firearm."

Without a pause, Cartwright did as he was bid, then took a step back. "Simms, I think we should—"

Simms held up his free hand, cutting Cartwright's words off. "Why'd he shoot your friends?"

The barman, identified as Toby, answered for the stricken Coulson, voice brittle, full of concern, even fear, "He asked them stuff and they were drunk. They couldn't answer and so, them not making much sense anyways, he shot them. Before anyone could do anything, he left."

"And you don't know where he went?"

"Heading east, I guess. Towards Bridger. The railroad has a main junction there now, the line that passes through here, and another heading to the northwest. It's more complete than this one."

Simms took a breath to speak when the saloon's doors snapped open and a gruff voice crackled across the room, "Put down that firearm, sir and move away. If not, you're a dead man."

Simms glanced over his shoulder and saw the words could well hold a great deal of truth. In the doorway was a well-dressed, serious gentleman in finely-tailored clothes, with two others behind him holding carbines. By the look of them and the assured way they held their aim, it seemed to Simms they knew what they were doing. With a smile, he held up the Dragoon with his forefinger far from the trigger and stepped away.

It was not his intention to die this day.

Nineteen

Towards the rail junction

"I won't dally with you, Detective," said Fergusson, pushing the telegram across the desk towards Simms. "You are who you say you are, and I hold Colonel Johnstone over at Bridger as a personal friend, so we have no issue. Not over your identity, at least."

"Well, that's reassuring." Simms shifted in the chair, craning his neck to scan across the two men standing over by the door. They no longer pointed their rifles, but they remained alert, ready to jump into action at the merest flicker from their boss.

"What still rankles me is how you have the audacity to walk into one of *my* saloons and pistol-whip one of *my* workers."

"If he hadn't swung the punch, it never would have happened."

"That's as maybe. The fact is, you pulled a gun and that, in my book, is a felony."

"I'm sure if you send another telegram to the headquarters of the Pinkerton Detective—"

"No, I don't think so, Detective." Fergusson stuck his thumbs into his waistband and inhaled deeply. "Coming into my camp and causing this amount of disturbance is simply not acceptable."

"I see. Well, you've already thrown my young companion into your jail, so what do you propose doing to me?"

"Jail isn't an option."

Simms frowned. The growing sense that something was very wrong with his situation gathered momentum, welling up from deep within in a rush, turning his throat dry and tight. He coughed. "So, what is?"

Fergusson smiled, shooting a glance towards his guards, one of whom chuckled, and said, "Detective Simms, I have a proposal. It's a simple one and if you accept, your young associate can live."

With his eyes hardening, his rage boiling, Simms struggled to remain in his chair. "What did you say?"

"I think you heard me. Do as I ask, Detective, and the young man will remain in jail until you return. If you refuse, he'll hang – in the morning."

A single oil lamp gave off a feeble light, but enough to pick out the details of the squat jailhouse. Rivulets of damp rolled down the bare, stone cell walls, and Cartwright sat huddled in the corner, knees drawn up to his chest, shivering. Cold and terror combined to envelop him in a cloak of pure misery and when he raised his head, dark smudges under his eyes gave him a wild, haunted look. Blood dripped from the corner of his mouth. They'd beaten him.

On the other side of the bars, Simms didn't like what he saw. "They gave you a hard time?"

"You could say that."

"You shouldn't have struggled."

"Oh, so this is my fault?"

"I'm not saying it was your—"

"I didn't do anything, Simms. They dragged me in here, then kicked and punched me to the ground. You want to see where their boots landed?" He went to pull up his shirt, anger replacing the fear.

"No, I believe you."

Cartwright blew out a breath. "Then damn you to hell."

Simms tried his best to sound convincing when he said, "It'll be all right, I promise you."

A thin smile, humorless and contemptuous, creased the young officer's haggard face. "You self-righteous bastard. I should have broken out on my own, like I said, and not listened to you!"

"You'd be already dead and you know it."

"At least I would have died trying."

"You're better off here, Lieutenant, believe me. Things will work out just fine."

"Oh, so what, I'm supposed to *believe* you, is that what this is, Detective? You tell me, what good am I going to do, sat here like some goddamned invalid?"

Close to the door, the big, lumbering guard shifted position and snorted, "Hurry up." Simms gave him a cursory glance before turning again to his young companion.

"Listen to me, Lieutenant. Everything is going to be fine. I'll be back within a few days. I'm going to Bridger with Fergusson. Understand me?"

"That's enough," said the guard, stepping forward. "Mr. Fergusson said you weren't supposed to—"

"Did you hear me, Lieutenant? With the water running so deep and all, you may want to know which way I'm heading."

Cartwright frowned in the gloom.

"We're going to catch a train," continued Simms, conscious of the shadow falling over him. "You get me? Just like the one you were travelling in. With your father. Remember? Remember what happened and *why* it happened?"

A hand came down on the detective's shoulder, the guard's voice rumbling with threat, "I told you, boy, that's enough."

Simms surrendered, his shoulders sagging and he turned away, the big guard prodding him in the back with a huge Colt Walker revolver. He crossed to the door and yanked it open, the wood screaming against rusted hinges.

"I'll be sure to use all the water I can get, Detective," called out Cartwright and Simms turned and raised his hand before the guard pushed him out into the night air.

Waiting outside were three riders, with Simms's own horse waiting patiently alongside. Fergusson sat in the middle, well wrapped up in a thick overcoat. He grinned as Simms approached. "When we reach the rail junction, I'll introduce you to the rest of the gang."

The guard pushed Simms forward. He went to his horse, put his foot in the stirrup and hauled himself up into the saddle. "I'll need my gun," he said.

"Not just yet, Detective. We'll ride through the night and be there by daybreak. If you behave yourself, I'll see what I can do. Winters," he nodded towards the guard, "you keep the boy alive. On our return, I'll reconsider the charges."

Simms bit his lip. "Charges? There are no charges, goddamn your sorry hide."

"Keep a civil tongue in your head, Simms, or I might forget that I'm a gentleman. The boy will remain unharmed so long as you do your part. You have my word."

Simms glared, but nevertheless remained silent. As Fergusson turned his horse away, Simms fell in between the railroad boss and the two other riders. The cold night air bit through his jacket and into his flesh, but he forced his discomfort aside and wondered once again what plans Fergusson had for him when they met up with the train outside of Fort Bridger.

* * *

They rode through the night, just as Fergusson had said, making steady progress across the plains. The sky was full of cloud, and somewhere far off thunder continued to rumble. When at last the storm finally came and the rain beat down upon them, Fergusson urged them on, bunching his shoulders against the downpour. Miserable, cold and soaked through, Simms made himself as small as he could in his saddle. Out here, in the open range, there would be little chance of escape. With no firearms, except for the small revolver still lashed to his leg, all he could do was wait and hope.

Fergusson didn't lay out the entire plan, but from the little he did reveal, Simms knew for certain he was being placed in a set-up. Towards what end, he could not yet guess. However, the situation grew clearer when the sky lightened and the sun struggled to cut through the grey clouds. The outline of the rail junction came into focus, and four men appeared from around a nearby bluff. Fergusson held up his hand and they all stopped and waited for the riders to draw close.

Horses snorted and nickered, stomping at the ground, growing anxious with the thunder all around them. Simms peered through the dull, half-light, trying his best to pick out Talpas, but the big man wasn't among them.

"You're on time," said the lead rider, pulling up his mount in front of Fergusson.

The tension fizzled between them and the horses, sensing it, grew restless, pulling on reins, struggling to get away.

Fergusson, tall in the saddle, ramrod straight, chuckled. "Did you ever doubt it?"

"I must admit, I had some fears, yes. Who's this?" The leader gestured with a leather-gloved hand towards Simms.

"Oh, just a little treat, something to sweeten up the entire proceedings."

"Don't you ever talk straight?"

"His name is Simms, and he's a Pinkerton detective."

A smaller, swarthy man behind the first snarled and brought his horse up closer. "Pinkerton? I've heard of them, Lol. From Chicago."

Lol stretched, his leather saddle creaking. "Chicago. You're a long way from home, mister. What you doing all the way out here?"

"Mr. Simms," interjected Fergusson, "is on the trail of some train robbers. He's come all the way out here to apprehend them."

"Has he by Christ?"

"Yes, he has."

"Why not kill him now," said the second one, pulling out his revolver and cocking it.

"Not so fast, Chato," said Lol, pausing to take a plug of tobacco from a little pouch wrapped around his pommel. He popped it into his mouth and chewed it up. "Tell us why he's here, Mr. Fergusson. We're all *dying* to know."

"Simple. He's going to help us guard the train as it heads out towards Brentville. When you and your boys hold it up, Mr. Simms here is going to get himself killed in the crossfire. And I'll be there, holding him as he dies, and I'll tell of how brave he was, how, after I'd hired him, he tried so hard to defend the well-earned wages of the workers over in Brentville. In other words, Lol, dear friend, he'll be my alibi and neither the law officers nor the railroad company will suspect a damned thing. All I need worry about is how much money I'm going to earn."

"You sorry bastard," said Simms.

Chuckling, Fergusson threw out his arms. "A perfect end to what will be a most perfect robbery."

The swarthy Mexican nodded towards Fergusson. "Is this man the source of the plan, Lol?"

"His name is Mister Fergusson, Chato. He's the owner of the railroad company."

"Not quite the owner, Lol," said Fergusson. He addressed Chato, holding the man's furious gaze. "I'm what is termed a Field Manager. The company pay me a paltry amount for recruiting and maintaining the workforce. It's a thankless job, my friend, and I'm sick to death of being taken for granted. I reckon I'm well overdue compensation."

"You almost got us killed last time," snarled Chato. "You said the train would be full of money."

"I thought it would be and I'm sorry for what happened."

"Perhaps they knew of your intentions," said Lol. "The company. You think they suspect anything?"

"Not a thing. How could they? No, it was a mistake and I intend to make sure it's not one that is repeated. That's why I'll be riding on board." He nodded towards Simms. "Together with the good detective, here."

Chato slowly eased off the hammer to his gun. "I want to be in the caboose with him," he said. "I'll kill him if anything goes wrong." He grinned. "I'll kill him anyway, detective shit."

"Seems like everyone's happy," said Lol. "Me and the boys will head on out to where we've set the ambush. If all goes well, we'll be a whole lot richer by this evening. You take care, Mr. Fergusson. Adios, Chato!"

He ripped off his hat, and slapping his horse's rump, spurred off across the plain, his two silent companions galloping behind him. Simms watched them pound away into the distance, Lol's hollering echoing across the vast prairie, and he wondered by this evening how many of them, including himself, would still be alive.

Twenty

Deep Water remembers

Out in the cold of the plain, Deep Water bunched up his knees and hugged himself close. He recalled how, when he and his father went out hunting one autumn day, not so unlike this one, the weather changed so quickly, and father believed they would die. 'Never to feel again the warmth of the sun on our faces.' If he tried hard enough, as he sat remembering, Deep Water thought he could hear his father's voice, low, reassuring, the voice of the man who loved him more than anyone else. Lifting his eyes, he tried to count the stars, to take his mind off the ghosts looming up at the edge of his mind. But despite his best efforts, his eyes grew bleary with tears as the memory of that terrible day returned.

They'd woken from a few short hours of freezing sleep, and led their ravaged ponies down into the small valley. On the horizon, the fires from the mines gave the sky an eerie red glow, as if damaged, or injured, its bruises virulent. Not wishing to encounter any men from the camp, they veered away to the west. As they turned, a single shot rang out across the vastness and hit father in the side of the neck. The ponies screamed, rearing up, and father's threw him and galloped off into the grey dawn. Deep Water struggled to keep his pony from bolting, but it was as if some terrible contagion seized it, pulling, bucking, striking out with its back legs to kick away the unknown terror falling down upon them.

Father rolled across the ground, hands clutching the pulsing wound, the blood spurting through his fingers. Desperate, Deep Water gave up the one-sided struggle and allowed the pony to run, but it had taken fewer than half a dozen steps before a second bullet hit her in the flank. It crumpled onto its forelegs, flinging Deep Water over its head. He tumbled, the sharp, broken ground cutting through his thin shirt, cutting flesh. He went with the forward momentum, managing to reach a small outcrop of rock, behind which he huddled, head down, gasping.

The pony gave a juddering breath, collapsed onto its side, and grew still.

Some way off, lying in the open, Father groaned, his legs thrashing, and Deep Water chanced a quick look. What he saw forced him to look again, longer this time, all danger from the unknown assailant forgotten and he watched as the man he loved died in front of his eyes.

He wept, biting his bottom lip so hard he drew blood. In an instant all that he knew, all that he cared for was gone. His world, shattered, would never be the same again. And what had warranted such an act? A simple hunting party, the two of them, out to find elk, anything to feed their family who waited in their camp a day's ride to the south.

"Father," he whispered, voice crackling with despair, hoping against hope his father may still be alive. "Father, *please*."

His father moved, a mere twitching of the leg, but enough to bring hope.

Deep Water cried out, in relief, confusion, desperation. He scrambled to his feet as his father's head lolled around to face him, mouth splitting into a thin smile.

"Deep…" he said, voice nothing more than a whimper. His eyes burned with the same intensity Deep Water had always known. A hand crawled, spider-like, across the dirt, a last act of supplication. "My son…"

Casting aside all thoughts for his own safety, Deep Water broke cover and stumbled forward, dropping to his knees, hands wiping away the hair from his father's brow, holding his face. Tears dripped down from Deep Water's nose to splash amongst the blood. "I'm here father."

"You must…" A forced swallow, eyes screwing up in agony, the enormity of the effort almost too much. He groaned again, tongue moistening trembling lips. "Try and make… Make your way…" His hand snaked out with amazing speed, and he gripped Deep Water's forearm, the strength of those fingers frightening. "Home."

From afar, a horse snickered and Deep Water snapped his face towards the sound. Through narrowed, moist eyes, he saw a rider dropping from his saddle. Two hundred paces, maybe more. With deliberate slowness, mechanical in his resolve, the man perched upon a large boulder and settled himself down across the top, the rifle evident.

Deep Water tore his eyes from the man and returned to his father, whose own eyes were staring, two black orbs with no light. Nothing.

He was dead.

And in that moment, Deep Water knew with utter certainty, his time in this world had also reached its end. Two hundred paces. Such a man with such a rifle would have no difficulty in putting the bullet wherever he wished.

Almost as if sensing it, becoming one with the surrounding air, feeling the sudden rush of heat, he swung away, the heavy caliber piece of lead shot missing its mark by a hair's breadth, to slap some paces away into the hard earth.

He ran, leaving his father behind. He thought he heard cursing from behind him and knew the killer would be hastily loading up another shot, but he didn't falter. Head down, swerving from left to right, he sprinted and didn't stop until he thought his lungs would burst, until his head pounded and his legs lost all feeling. He fell face down onto the earth, gasping for air, muscles screaming, pain like a knife piercing his side. How far he had run he couldn't say, but he hoped it was far enough. He lay still, aware only of the growing heat as the day grew brighter, the sun higher. Taking a breath, he raised his head and took a look around him. Nothing stirred across the open plain, or amongst the scattered clusters of rock and gorse. No waiting killer lurked, no muzzle flash. After a few more breathless moments, he pushed himself to a sitting position and continued on his way, stumbling forward, body shaking. Amongst a clump of coarse grass, he saw his pony grazing, becalmed, and he wanted to cry.

No tears.

Not now. Not for his father, not for his life. No. Only one thought burned its way through every living second. Revenge.

Twenty one

Breakout

Vinnie Winters sat slumped in the swivel chair behind the large desk, half asleep, wrapped in a thick blanket. Across the room, in the tiny cell, the young Lieutenant snored. Outside, nothing stirred, an occasional dog barking from far away. Shifting position, trying to get comfortable, Vinnie silently cursed Fergusson for not choosing him to go across country to intercept the train with the others. He longed for adventure, something to break the monotony of a drab, dull life. Anything to bring change.

A sudden gust of wind caused the door to rattle, the sound of grit trailing across the wooden slats outside on the boardwalk strangely eerie in the stillness. Vinnie, numb with cold, pulled up his collar. He thought he should try and light the little stove in the far corner, but the thought of having to spend so long stacking up hunks of woods and kindling in the stark chill of the jail was too much. Better to snuggle deeper into his coat and blanket. The morning would bring warmth once more. A few more hours of discomfort was all he had to endure. He closed his eyes, hopeful of sleep.

Without warning, the door tore open, as if of its own volition, rusted hinges squealing, and slammed against the wall. Vinnie sat up, grappling for his gun. The wind howled, sending an icy blast into the jailhouse, blowing out the spluttering light of the single oil lamp on the desk. Squinting through the gloom, Vinnie focused on the scene of the night beyond, shadowy shapes of buildings across the street breaking up the vista. But nothing moved outside, nothing of any substance at least, so he stood, dropping the blanket, and sending out a smattering of curses, went to the door to close it.

The shadow fell over him and although he saw it, he was unable to react fast enough. The knife went into his body just below the breastbone, the assailant driving the blade ever deeper, forcing Vinnie back into the room, arm flailing, mouth opening in a silent scream of terror. As he fell back against the desk, the breath rushing out of him, his revolver slipped out of his fingers and the assailant, no more than a blur of blackness, withdrew the knife and struck again, and again. Vinnie threw out both hands, in a vain, pathetic attempt to ward off further attacks. He died, bewildered and bloodied.

"Oh my God."

Deep Water stood up, alert, checking the room for other guards, and shot the now fully awake Cartwright a glance. "Quiet."

The scout took the bunch of keys from the dead Vinnie's belt, padded over to the cell door and fitted key after key into the lock, hands trembling, pausing to look to the main door every so often.

Finally, letting out a whoop of triumph, he found the correct one and turned the lock. Without waiting, Cartwright ripped open the door and moved to the rack of rifles on the adjacent wall. He took down his own carbine, checked the load, and only then allowed his eyes to rest upon the ghastly sight of Vinnie's corpse.

"How many others?" asked the scout.

"I'm not sure. They rode out towards—"

"I know. I saw them. They have Simms."

"They mean to use him as the means to give Fergusson an alibi. That bastard's behind the whole damned thing, probably has been all along. I always wondered how the robbers knew the train we were travelling on was carrying the wages. Now I know."

Stooping down, Deep Water took the revolver from beside Vinnie's corpse and put it in his waistband. "We must go. I have the horses waiting outside, already saddled. If we ride hard we can catch them."

"They have about four or five hours on us."

"Yes. We will do what we can."

So they rode out of that bleak and desolate place into the cold night, some hours before the miners trudged to work, or shopkeepers opened up their shutters and swept their entrances. Nobody stirred in the chill of the early morning, with the sky leaden, the only sound the pounding of two horses, disappearing out across the endless plain.

Twenty two

Plans are set

A little under a year before, when Simms alighted the train at its terminus, a small, indistinct town, the population small, the atmosphere verging on sleepy. Since then, workers, toiling in the heat of summer, and the intense, numbing cold of winter, extended the line, laying the iron rails over the land, stretching it for miles, ever deeper into the interior. Along the way, temporary camps sprang up, and the evidence of such places punctuated the route, the detritus of human existence scattered and discarded in every direction. At one point, the rail tracks split, one section disappearing to the northwest, and it was here that Lol and his companions had set their trap. Using heavy rocks, pieces of timber, and one or two broken carts taken from one of the camps, they erected a barrier across the rails, clearly visible to the driver of the approaching train. Satisfied, they slinked off towards a nearby gulch, towering rocks erupting from the iron-grey land, allowing them excellent cover. There, they settled down, checked their firearms, ate hard tack, and stretched out to catch some rest.

Away to the east, a group of riders rode into the town of Solemnity, a new town emerging alongside the tracks. At this time of the morning, people were stretching themselves to welcome a new day. Already, carpenters and painters were busily working on recently erected buildings, businesses were opening, townsfolk crossing a single street, which was little more than a dirt track. The riders reined in their mounts behind the rail station and dropped down from their saddles. On the other side of the squat ticket office, a locomotive belched steam, passengers milling around on the platform, preparing to enter the three waiting carriages. The driver leaned out from his cab, face awash with grime, and dragged an oily cloth across his brow. Sauntering up to him, the guard exchanged a few words. Neither of them noticed the men clumping behind them. In their hands they held carbines, and around their waists holstered revolvers. Only one man stood unarmed. A tall, hard-faced man, square-jawed, his eyes locked towards the distance. If anyone had paused to study him more closely, they may have noticed the grizzled, swarthy man beside him, with a drawn revolver in his hand, and they may have wondered why. But then the whistle blew from the locomotive, a gust of white steam accompanying it, with the guard's voice yelling, "All aboard!" So no one noticed and the men stepped onto the train, the best dressed of them with the swarthy man and the unarmed one alongside, making their way to the caboose.

No one noticed. Later, many wished they had.

The brakeman in the caboose looked up from sorting out a pile of boxes and packages, raising a single eyebrow as the men came in, all hot and sweaty.

"You be Mr. Fergusson?"

"I am. And these are the guards, as arranged."

The brakeman nodded, motioning towards a carbine propped up against a nearby corner. "I was told to arm myself."

"Always wise," said Fergusson, pulling back his jacket to reveal two Navy Colts holstered at his belt, butts pointing inwards. "It is my hope we will not encounter mischief, but I have it on good intelligence that such an eventuality is likely." He looked across at Simms and Chato. "My friends here will position themselves at the rear. I have other men in the forward carriages." There was a sudden jerk as the locomotive released its brakes. Fergusson stumbled, reaching out to brace himself against the wall, and Simms caught him. For a moment, they stared into one another's eyes, then Simms smiled and the train lurched forward. A uniformed guard clambered aboard, breathing hard, and Chato gripped Simms shoulder and pulled him away. Fergusson grunted, "Thank you, Detective."

The guard gave a glance outside before sliding the caboose door closed, the locomotive picking up speed, the air filled with the smell of steam and the sound of the shunting, huffing engine. "You gentlemen the extra guards?"

"This is Mr. Fergusson, Bill," said the brakeman, straightening himself. "There may be some trouble later, so he suspects."

"I see," said Bill. "Seems to be a might too much trouble on these lines as of late, if you ask me."

"I entirely agree," said Fergusson, "that is why we have a detective with us, from the Pinkerton Agency in Chicago."

Bill's eyes travelled over Simms, who stood rooted to the spot, eyes betraying no emotion. "I ain't heard of no such agency. Nor detectives. Seems to me we don't need no detecting, only the apprehension of the sonsofbitches that rob our trains."

"Well, that's what we're here to do, Bill." Fergusson stepped across and patted the guard on the arm, "I have engaged Mr. Simms to help us arrest the criminals who are robbing my good men back in camp of their well-earned wages. If they strike today, we shall have them – fear not my friend."

Bill considered Fergusson for a moment, grunted, then moved across to the large, iron safe, as tall as a man, set against the far wall. By now the train was reaching its cruising speed and Bill swayed like a drunkard as he stooped down and tried the safe door. "Well, whatever does happen, they won't be breaking inside this."

"You have the key, I trust?"

Bill turned, frowning. "Key? This needs no key, sir. It has a combination lock, brand new, guaranteed to withstand explosives, acids and drilling."

Fergusson, trying hard not to swallow too hard, rubbed his chin and took a breath. "I see. I knew nothing about this."

"No, well, it was only fitted two days ago. The rail company took it upon themselves to introduce whatever measures they believed necessary to thwart any would-be attackers."

"Now, isn't that just fine and dandy," grinned Simms. "Guaranteed against explosives and acids, eh?"

"And drilling."

Chuckling, Simms pushed Chato aside and marched to the rear of the caboose. He stepped outside and leaned on the iron railings, staring down at the blur of the tracks, not caring what Fergusson's reaction might be at the news about the safe. It struck him that perhaps the rail company had their suspicions concerning the so-called Field Manager Fergusson's loyalties. He couldn't help but smile as he set his mind on what he had to do, and when he had to do it.

Chato stepped up next to him, hawked and spat over the side. "When it begins, you die."

"Might be you'll be the one dying, friend."

Stiffening, Chato struck out his hand with the gun and pressed it into Simms side, "I'll kill you now, you bastard."

"Oh? And what will the witnesses say about that?" Simms shook his head, calm, nonchalant. "Put your gun away before there's an accident and you find yourself staring up into the eyes of the Devil himself."

Chatos' eyes flashed white in his burnished face. "What the hell does that mean, you gringo sonofabitch?"

"It means if you don't take that gun out of my side, I'll ram it up your ass." He winked. "You have three seconds before I kill you and that sorry piece of trash Fergusson back inside."

"You would not dare."

"Try me. One…"

Within a blink, Chato stepped back and holstered his gun. He turned to look out across the plain and the rapidly diminishing smudge on the horizon that was the town of Solemnity. His voice trembled with barely-contained rage when he spoke. "I will enjoy killing you."

"Yeah. I'm sure." He winked. "Fantasies are like that. Trouble is, reality is never quite as exciting."

Leaving a non-plussed Chato to try and unravel Simms words, the detective went back inside as the train began to move up a steady incline, its speed slowing somewhat. Fergusson sat on a small poop-seat at the far end of the caboose, seemingly dozing, his chin resting on his chest. Crossing over to a low bench, Simms took a drink from one of the canteens there. A sudden noise caused him to turn, instinctively going for his gun, which of course, wasn't there. The brakeman was on his knees, gathering up a load of fallen parcels, the lurch of the locomotive no doubt causing them to fall. Simms went over to help, catching Chato staring from the open exit. But the Mexican, sullen, bored and disinterested, quickly turned away to study the passing landscape once more.

"I notice you're not armed, Detective."

Simms started at the man's words, delivered in a whisper. He shot a glance to Chato, who was out of earshot and remained standing outside, and then to Fergusson. The man hadn't stirred. Simms answered in his own, low tones. "They took them."

Nodding, as if in total understanding, the brakeman continued to collect up the parcels, but much more carefully now. "I thought as much. I've been watching them, especially that Mexican. You're not guards at all, are you?"

"No. There's going to be a hold-up, and when it starts it will get very messy, very quickly." The guard frowned. "They mean to shoot me dead, using my death as a means for Fergusson over there to have a watertight alibi. He's the mastermind."

"I have a pistol, as well as the carbine," said the guard, placing the last of the parcels into its allotted pigeonhole. "I'll leave it on the far side of the safe. When the shooting starts, it'll help. I'll take my carbine and do what I can."

"Thanks, but not wishing to give offence, these are a vicious bunch. I'm not sure if you could—"

"I served in the War so I know a lot about killing – too much, if I'm honest. I'd hoped that by taking this job I could leave that part of my life behind me. Seems I was wrong."

"We all have past lives we'd rather forget about. Unfortunately, it isn't always so easy." He smiled, patted the brakeman on the arm and stood up, making a big show of stretching his back. Chato turned, sneering, but only for a moment.

The connecting door to the rest of the train opened and the guard came through. Fergusson stirred, yawned and blinked several times before he caught sight of Simms and grinned. He reached for his fob watch, attached to a chain draped across his midriff, and opened the timepiece up. "Not long now, detective. Best get ourselves ready."

"Get ready for what?" asked the guard.

Fergusson shrugged, "Why Bill, the junction, of course. We'll be rattling over some points. We wouldn't want the good detective to lose his footing and fall over onto his sorry ass, would we?"

The guard looked from Fergusson to Simms and back again. "Junction's around five minutes from here. We'll be slowing down soon, so there should be no jolting."

"No, no, I'm sure. I was merely commenting on the fact that—"

From nowhere came a loud blast from the locomotive's whistle. The guard spun on his heels, and motioned towards the brakeman. "Sounds like we might be making a stop, Clem."

Clem nodded and stepped towards the rear entrance, with Chato standing there, watching. "I have to make my way forward across the roof and twist the brake wheels." The Mexican grunted and stepped aside, allowing Clem to reach down to grab a large club propped up in the corner, next to the carbine.

Another shrill blast, followed by several more, and the brakeman stopped, snapped his head around. "What the hell is going on, Bill, do you have any idea?"

"Something on the line maybe," said Bill and went over to the large sliding door. He grunted with the effort of pulling it back giving him sufficient space to peer out. "Oh, my good God Almighty."

"What is it?" asked Clem, making to move back inside.

Simms stepped away, watching how Fergusson rose slowly to his feet, motioning towards Chato to come in from outside, whilst pulling back his coat to give easier access to his firearms. The Mexican gave a short nod, hand hovering over his gun.

Chancing another look outside, Bill turned to Clem, face serious. "It looks like something on the line. I can't make it out, but you'd best get on top, Clem, and knock on the brakes."

As if to lend more weight to his words, the whistle gave yet another, far longer blast.

Fergusson edged closer to Bill, his grin broadening. "Just take another look, would you please? I'm kinda curious as to what it might be."

Bill grunted and did so, leaning out as far as he could, left hand gripping the door edge. Without hesitating, Fergusson swung in behind and pushed the guard out of the caboose. The man screamed and for one awful moment clung on to the side paneling as the rest of him flayed about outside, the moving ground beneath him hard and dangerous. With a dismissive, somewhat impatient grunt, Fergusson slammed the sliding door shut on the guard's fingers. A muffled scream followed and Fergusson leaned back on the door, taking in a few deep breaths.

"What in the hell did you—"

Clem's question was cut off by Chato, who strode up to him and put the muzzle of his revolver into the brakeman's neck.

"You need to apply the brakes, friend," said Fergusson.

"I'll not do a goddamned thing to help you, you miserable son of a—"

"If you don't, my Mexican friend here will kill you."

"And the train will go right through whatever it is blocking the rail, you idiot."

"Yes, no doubt. So the train will derail, I shouldn't wonder." He smiled, placing his hands on his hips and regarded Clem with much amusement. "Wanna be responsible for the almost certain deaths of so many innocent passengers?"

"You'd best do it," put in Simms, who stood with his arms folded, appearing somewhat bored with everything.

"Now there speaks sense," said Fergusson.

Clem's shoulders sagged, the fight leaving him. "All right, but not for you, not for *any* of you." He gave Simms a vicious glare. "For the passengers."

Stepping aside, Chato gave Clem room to trudge towards the rear entrance.

"One thing puzzles me," said Simms, watching the brakeman preparing to climb up onto the caboose roof.

Chuckling, Fergusson checked his fob watch again. "Only one?"

"How do you plan to open the safe?"

"The combination will be here somewhere. If it's not, I'll send a telegram back to Bridger, ask them for it. They'll trust me."

"You really are one rat-assed, dust-guzzling idiot," cackled Clem, and he put his foot on the first rung of the narrow, iron ladder which would take him to the roof.

"Watch your mouth," spat Chato.

"Why do you say that, friend?" Fergusson cocked his head. "You don't believe me when I say the authorities back in Bridger trust me?"

"No," replied Clem, laughing much more freely now, "the reason I say it is simple. Bill had the combination. In his coat pocket. And you just threw the poor bustard out of the train!"

Twenty three

Tracks in the dirt

In the improving daylight they stopped, Deep Water slipping from his pony and immediately dropping to his knees, his eyes roaming over the ground. "I thought I'd lost the tracks in the dark, but my instincts were good." He stood up and faced the distant horizon. "For now, their tracks head in the direction of Fort Bridger, but I do not think that is their destination."

"They'll find a place where the train will have to slow."

"Or force it to stop."

"A barricade, you mean? Something across the rails, like a tree or rocks?"

"Yes. Perhaps." The scout swung himself up onto the back of his pony. "You need to rest?"

"I rested enough in that damned cell. We'll keep going until we catch up with them."

But when Deep Water next reined in his pony a few hours later, it wasn't because the gang was close, but because of what he saw in the dirt. Again, he got down, examining the evidence with more than his usual care. After a few moments, he shook his head, the point of his tongue pressing against his teeth, concern written in every line of his face. "There is another rider."

Joining him, Cartwright got down next to the Indian and frowned at the scuffed-up ground. "I don't see anything except a few hoof prints. How the hell can you read all this?"

Deep Water didn't answer, setting his gaze towards a group of low-lying hills and craggy outcrops some distance to his left. "This group, they ride off towards those rocks, and someone follows them. Another group, they continue straight ahead. Towards Bridger."

"That'll be the group Simms is with. They mean to get him on board the train." He stood up, put his good hand into the small of his back and stretched out his spine. "Damn, I'm cramped. I ain't used to being in the saddle for so long."

"I am going to the hills."

"What? You can't – we have to help Simms!"

"Simms can look after himself. Better than most. And I think this other rider, he is the man with the long-rifle."

"The sharpshooter? How can you tell that?"

"I can't. But it is what I believe, and if it so, then I am going to the hills. It is a good place for him to wait, and shoot with his long-rifle."

He went to move, but Cartwright stepped in his way, hand up. "Hold on, Deep Water, we had a plan. To get to the train and stop it from being robbed."

"We can still do that. The men who have gone to the hills, they will be the group who will block the line."

"That's just a guess."

"Why else would they split? Look." He pointed to the tracks, which ran off towards Bridger. "You can see there. That is where Simms has gone, so the others," he turned and pointed this time towards the hills in the distance, "they went that way."

"With the sharpshooter following? I don't know. You think he's going to do what he did last time, take some potshots, kill the guards?"

"Or kill Simms. How else to kill a man as resourceful as the detective if not from a distance?"

"Jesus, you could be right." Cartwright chewed furiously at his bottom lip whilst kneading his forehead with his fingers. "Goddamnit, this is a sorry situation." He dropped his hand and held the scout's gaze. "I get the feeling there is something you're not telling me. A feeling I've had since the first moment I met you. Sure, you came along to help Simms track those bastards, but there's something else." The Indian's black eyes remained empty of emotion. "I think you should tell me, before we decide what to do next."

"I have already decided. I am going to the hills."

Cartwright's hand dropped to the holstered revolver at his side. "We're not going anywhere until you give me a good reason to follow you."

"I have told you the reason. They will be blocking the rails. And the other one, he will be setting up his rifle."

"Fair enough, but you tell me this – why did you ride off after the sharpshooter in such a rush after he'd killed those Indians some days ago? And why did you speak with the wounded man you left behind? What did you say to him?"

"I asked him which way the long-hair went, and he told me. He also told me his name."

"And what has that to do with anything?"

"Because I want to know the name of the man who will die under my knife." Deep Water's breathing grew ragged and he looked away, but not before Cartwright noticed the tears welling up. "Some fifteen months or so ago, I was hunting with my father. For days we had ridden across the prairie, searching for game, but the lack of rain forced every living thing deeper and deeper into the interior. We came across some settlements as we rode. They were old gold and silver mines, and we moved away because we did not wish to meet with anyone in such places. My people knew that the mines had hired men to kill any of us who ventured close. And then, as we set our sights in the opposite direction, the shot hit my father and he fell. I tried to…" He blew out his cheeks and looked again at Cartwright, making no effort now to disguise his heartbreak, two trails of tears running freely down his cheeks. "I saw him, the man who killed my father, and I ran. I ran, not because of fear, but because I knew I could never get close enough to kill him before he killed me. So, I ran. And when I found my pony, which had bolted, I made my way to where the rest of my family was camped. They were all dead."

Stunned, Cartwright didn't know what to say, and he allowed the Indian's words to hang in the air and waited.

"My mother lay across the camp fire, her body smoldering, the great hole in her back a witness to the heavy bullet which had torn through her and taken her life."

"The sharp shooter?"

Deep Water nodded. "We all knew how afraid the whites were of us, thinking we would attack them. These hired men, they ranged far and long and killed any they came across – Utes, Shoshone, even Comanche who had travelled far from their lands in search of food. And us. Kiowa. The killers, they do not distinguish, nor do they care. This one, the longhair, he had walked into our camp after shooting my mother and murdered my brother and sister at close range. I found their tiny bodies hidden amongst some gorse bushes where they had run in terror from him. My brother was twelve summers, my sister eight. Ever since, I have searched for him, often losing his trail, but always sensing how close he was. And now he is here."

"It's changed you, hasn't it, this longing for vengeance?"

Their eyes met and something passed between them, a shared anguish, an understanding. "You speak words of truth, Lieutenant. I am nineteen summers old, yet I feel fifty. My life holds nothing else for me but to see him dead, the longhair. So I go to the mountains, to seek him out and kill him."

Cartwright grunted, "Our destinies are linked, Deep Water, because if the man who killed my father is also there then we shall both have our vengeance this day."

And together they turned their horses to the north and headed across the plain.

Twenty four

Shootout

Lol stood on a raised outcrop, mouth chomping on a plug of tobacco, overseeing Spiro and Dwayne who struggled and sweated with their labors some feet below. He didn't hear the approach of the other man until the low cough snapped him into action and he turned, in a half-crouch, gun coming up from out of its holster. He froze in the action of pulling back the hammer.

"Hello Lol."

Grinning, Talpas, with his own revolver already cocked, stood some ten feet away and appeared relaxed, nonchalant almost, but Lol knew the man's capabilities, so he remained still. "I thought you were dead."

"Well, I ain't and you was wrong. Slip that gun of yours back in its holster, Lol, before I plug you."

Without arguing, Lol did as Talpas said. Below, the others continued hefting large rocks and pieces of rotten tree trunk across the rails, unaware that some thirty or so paces from where they worked, death may have come a-calling.

Talpas moved across to another rock, out of sight of the two brothers, and sat down, his revolver trained unerringly towards Lol's midriff. "Now then, let's get straight to it, shall we?"

"Straight to *what*?"

"Perhaps you'd mind telling me where the money is. *My* money."

"*Your* money? What in the name of God Almighty are you talking about?"

"Don't play the meek and innocent with me, Lol. You know damned well what I mean – the money we took from the last robbery, you double-crossing piece of shit."

"I ain't no double-crosser. We thought you was dead."

"Why d'you think that, Lol? The plan was to make for the hideout and divide up the takings. You weren't there. I'm suspecting you and that Mexican scumbag decided to make off with the money all by your lonesome."

"That's not so. We had to make other plans. So we waited for you, in town. When you didn't show, we—"

"Assumed we was all dead. Harris, Ned. Me."

"That's right."

"Well, thing is, Lol, them other two is dead. I killed 'em."

Lol sucked in his breath. "Then that was a mighty stupid thing to do, Talpas. They didn't know where the money was."

"No. But they said you did, Lol. And, I believed 'em. Men tend not to lie when they're about to meet their maker." He tilted his head. "So, I'll ask you just the once. *Where* is my money?"

"It's gone."

A dark look came over Talpas' face and his grin turned to a snarl. "I do so hope you're lying, Lol. That money is mine. I want my share."

"Jesus, is that what this is all about? We spent it, all of it, that's why we're here now. To hold up another."

"You *spent* it? What do you take me for, Lol, some sort of addled, brain-dead idiot?" He stood up, any semblance of restraint replaced by something dangerous and unpredictable. He crossed the distance between them and pistol-whipped Lol across the jaw, dropping him to the ground, where he lay, groaning and rolling in the dirt, clutching at his face. "Don't fuck with me, you bastard. There is no way you could have spent all that money!"

Lol groaned and propped himself up on one elbow, whilst dabbing at his broken mouth with a fingertip. "I'll kill you."

"What? From the next life?"

"The money wasn't anywhere near as much as we was told. It was a few measly thousand."

"You're lying."

"Am I?" He sniggered and spat a mouthful of blood onto the ground. "Why in the hell do you think we're here? We're holding up another train and this time I'm assured we'll reap great benefits."

"Assured? Who the hell is assuring you? The same dumb fuck who told you about the last train and the treasures it held?"

"He explained. It was all a big misunderstanding. I believe him."

"That makes you a bigger fool than I ever thought. Dear God Almighty, if you're lying to me, I'll kill you, you sonofabitch."

"If you let us do our job, you'll see I ain't lying."

"When it's over, you give me what is rightfully mine."

Before Lol could offer up a suitable retort, a voice cried out from below. "*Lol! Lol, we think we're done down here. Come and take a look.*"

Talpas snapped his head up. From where he was, he couldn't see the owner of the voice, so he stepped up onto the outcrop where Lol had stood, and shot the first person he saw down below in the chest.

"Oh no," wailed Lol, rolling onto his back. "You fucking idiot, you'll ruin everything."

From below, the sound of the second man came, screaming indistinct words, his tone one of disbelief mingled with shock and grief.

But Talpas was no longer listening to anything. He aimed his revolver with extreme care, holding his breath, one eye closing.

From somewhere deep within, borne out of fear or anger – or both – Lol dragged up the strength to move. With his mouth alive with pain, his entire head ringing from the blow of the revolver, Lol launched himself towards Talpas' legs, slamming into the big man with all the strength he could muster, and bundled him over the edge of the rocky outcrop. The revolver went off, but Lol neither knew nor cared if it had found its target. Gripping Talpas by the material of his buckskin trousers, he held on to the sharpshooter as they both went careering over the edge, tumbling down the incline, locked together in a mad whirl of desperation.

At the foot of the rise, the two bodies hit the ground with a bone-jarring impact. Talpas took the brunt of the fall, allowing Lol to rear up. Lifting Talpas by the lapels, Lol butted the sharpshooter hard in the nose. The big man squealed, blood spouting, and Lol butted him a second time, quickly following up with a knee rammed into his groin. Talpas, bleating like a baby now, sagged in Lol's arms, retching loudly and Lol finished it with a swinging left into the big man's temple.

"Son of a bitch," rasped Lol, bent double, gulping in air, eyes never leaving the inert mass of the sharp shooter sprawled across the dirt, vomit and blood trailing from his shattered face.

"Oh sweet Jesus, Lol."

Turning, Lol saw Dwayne on the ground, tears cascading down his face, holding Spiro's head as if it were some delicate possession, to be protected and nurtured. But Spiro was beyond any of that. His lifeless eyes stared out from a chalk white face, the horrible sheen of death covering every feature. And Dwayne wept and Lol stood, as if in a daze, not knowing what to think or what to say until the first blast of the approaching train's whistle snapped him out of his indecision, forcing him into action.

"We gotta get into position," he said, reaching down to Talpas and relieving the unconscious regulator of his guns. He went over to the makeshift barricade, placed across the rails by Dwayne and his brother, and peering down the line, saw the stream of smoke from the oncoming locomotive. "It's slowing, but we ain't got long. When it stops, we get on board and do what we need to do."

"I ain't going no place, Lol," cried Dwayne, stroking his brother's hair, "not now I ain't."

"You'll fucking well move, Dwayne, or I'll shoot you right here."

"Best do it, then, Lol, 'cause I ain't moving. That bastard shot Spiro, and I aim to kill him. But not now, not whilst he's sleeping. I want to see the look on his face when I put a bullet in his brain."

"After is when you do that, Dwayne. When we is done with robbing the goddamned train!"

He stepped across and took Dwayne by the shoulder of his jacket, hauling the spluttering youth to his feet. "Afterwards, we'll bury Spiro and you can kill that sonofabitch with as many bullets as you please. But we take the train first, Dwayne. I can't do this on my own, damn it." He winced as he gingerly touched the swelling along his jawline. "God knows I owe that bastard myself, but he's all yours Dwayne, I promise you. Just get your shit together and help me get aboard the train when it stops."

For a moment, Lol believed Dwayne might refuse. He stood rigid, his face ablaze with fury, glaring towards Talpas, whose moans were growing in volume as he slowly regained consciousness.

"All right, Lol. All right." Dwayne sniffed loudly, nodding his head and Lol released him from his grip.

Turning, Lol moved again towards Talpas, who had taken up coughing and spluttering, clearing his throat and mouth of the blood and bile accumulating there. "I'll put him to sleep again, the bastard, then we'll—"

The first shot echoed through the cluster of rocks, a bullet pinging off a nearby boulder. Yelling, Lol dived for cover as a second lump of red-hot lead smacked into the ground where he had stood. He scrambled behind some cover, tearing his gun from his holster, but not daring to raise his head until he knew for certain from where the shots originated.

Unlike him, however, Dwayne decided on a different course, fanning his own revolver like someone possessed, firing off ill-aimed, wild shots into the surroundings. With his gun quickly spent, he whirled around, screaming, "Throw me one of his guns, Lol, I think I—"

He never reached the end of his sentence, words cut off as the back of his head exploded in a great red cloud of blood and brain. Lol watched as Dwayne crumpled to his knees then toppled onto his side, and remained still, lying next to his brother.

The locomotive's whistle blasted closer still and Lol squeezed his eyes shut and cursed all the gods that had ever been, his life, the world, anything he could think of. For it to end here, like this, amongst nameless rocks in a God-forsaken land, with no one left to remember him or say his name. Damn them all, each and every one.

He climbed to his feet, pulling out one of Talpas' guns from his waist, and with his own gun in the other hand, stepped out into the open, both revolvers blazing. He didn't know who the killers were, or where they were. He no longer cared. Life, for him, held nothing more. Not a day, an hour, or minute. Everything he ever was, ended here.

Twenty five

The railroad hold up

"What in the name of good God is that?" demanded Fergusson, stepping back from the open door, eyes everywhere, voice cracking in confusion.

"Sounded like gunfire," said Simms, standing with his back against the opposite side of the caboose, motionless, arms folded.

Shooting him a fierce look, Fergusson strode through the car to where Chico stood, neck straining, peering up to the roof of the caboose. "Go topside with the brakeman and find out what the hell is happening down the line."

Chico gaped. "Go topside? Are you crazy? I'm not going up there, not for you, not for anyone."

"Do it," snapped Fergusson, tugging out his revolver. "I'll kill you if you don't."

"You be careful who you're threatening, Mr. Fergusson." Chico grinned. "You haven't even eased back the hammer on your piece."

Fergusson blinked, looked down and Chico threw out his right fist and smashed it squarely into the older man's face. Yelping, Fergusson staggered backwards and Chico followed, hitting him hard in the guts, bending him double, and swiftly following it up with a left cross which felled Fergusson to the floor.

"Chico."

The Mexican turned to answer the mention of his name, and in that single moment, knew the situation was about to change.

Simms stood, taking his chance whilst the Mexican beat Fergusson to the ground to pick up the revolver the brakeman had placed behind the safe. Smiling, Simms shot Chico twice in the chest, sending him spinning backwards to smack into the caboose's far side. Flattened against the woodwork, the Mexican's body slid lifeless to the floor, blood smearing from his wounds across the slats, tracking the journey of his fall.

Acting quickly now, Simms went over to the still open door and peered out. The wheels of the train squealed as the brakeman did his job, and the whole train slowed down to a virtual crawl. He saw the barricade, but not the waiting robbers. Then, as he watched the tell-tale puffs of weapons discharging in the thick, fetid air, he grinned for he knew who was there. Cartwright and Deep Water.

Turning, he crossed to Fergusson and lifted him to his feet. Bloodied and bruised, the railroad manager sagged in Simms grip, semi-conscious. Simms shook him. "Fergusson, wake up you sorry piece of shit." He released him and Fergusson crumpled, body jarring against the wall where he sat, slumped beside Chato's corpse. Moaning, head lolling on his chest, his mouth drooled with blood and saliva.

"I'll watch him," said the brakeman, reappearing from outside. He stooped down and pulled Chato's gun from the dead man's holster. "You do what you need to do, Detective."

Nodding, Simms returned to the door, measuring the distance from it to the ground. He took one more look back at the brakeman and said, "Thanks, Bill," then jumped. The slow speed of the locomotive, inching along by now, meant the impact when Simms tumbled over the ground was considerably less than it might have been. Even so, his recently damaged shoulder took the brunt of the fall, the muscle of his shoulder screaming out in protest, forcing him up into a ball where he remained for some time, gritting his teeth, waiting for the pain to pass.

Hissing with agony, he flexed his muscle and massaged it with the fingers of his other hand. Not dislocated this time, but still sore. Cursing, he took off across the open ground, keeping close to the track, in the direction of the shootout occurring amongst the rising rocks and hills some two hundred paces ahead.

From his cab, the train driver leaned out and shouted to Simms as he trundled passed, "What the hell do I do?"

"Stop and wait," shouted Simms in reply, slowing down to nothing more than a stagger, breathing hard. His shoulder buzzed with pain and he knew, if he got out of this alive, he'd need medical help. But not now. Now, he needed every fiber, joint and tendon working, because up ahead he saw a man stepping out in full view, with guns in his hands and he was working the hammers, firing in every direction.

"That's him," snarled Cartwright aloud, chancing a look from behind his rocky cover, "God damn it all, there he is!"

He went to stand, but Deep Water gripped his arm, forcing him back down. "He'll kill you, Lieutenant."

As if to confirm the scout's warning, two bullets smacked into the rock, pinging off in opposite directions. Careless of the danger, however, Cartwright tore himself free, and stood up.

The man with the two guns stopped, his face a black mask of fury, eyes wild, mouth a thin sneer. Cartwright took a step. His own revolver was in his waistband, his carbine, which was empty, he discarded. At no more than twenty paces apart, Cartwright came to a halt.

"Do you remember me?"

The man with the two guns frowned. Cartwright took another step.

"You should remember me, you bastard. You put a gun to my head before you shot my father dead."

"Your father?"

"We were on board the last train you robbed. You recall what you did?"

The man sniggered. "Ah yes, I remember it now. You were in uniform then, as I recall. I shot you. I thought you were dead."

"You ruined my arm, you bastard, and my chance of a career in the army. But you did more than that. You took my father's life, destroying my mother's, and now I'm here to kill you for what you did."

"You are? Well, bully for you, you stupid shit." And the man's guns came up and the hammers fell.

For some time, Talpas lay on the ground, battling to regain his strength. Lol's fists hit him like a blacksmith's hammer, so heavy, so solid. He didn't think anyone had ever punched him so hard in all his life. He'd underestimated the train robber, and that was something he didn't usually do. He'd almost paid for the mistake with his life, but now it was Lol's mistake which gave him the opportunity to escape. The mistake of not killing him. So, waiting for the right moment, he rolled over onto his stomach and crawled away, slithering between the rocks until he was well clear of any gunshot, aimed or otherwise. Only when he was safely out of range did he climb to his feet, still groggy, and weave his way towards his horse.

Taking a moment to rest his head against the saddle, he settled his breathing before reaching for his rifle. With great care, he checked the load, gathered more powder, lead and percussion caps, then set off on a steady climb up the nearby rock face.

Injuries forced him to take his time, his breathing coming in rattling gulps. He knew his nose was broken and his eyes, streaming with tears, were clearly badly bruised. He slipped more than once, desperate to hold on, measuring each step with consummate care.

Reaching some level ground, he checked the sights of his rifle and settled himself into position. The area chosen allowed him a clear view of the railway line, the now-stationary locomotive, and the standoff between Lol and another man some distance below. What took most of his attention, however, was another man running across the open plain. If he had time, Talpas would fit the long, slim telescopic sight over the top of the rifle barrel and home in on this advancing stranger. But time was something he had precious little of, so he took aim on Lol. As the most dangerous, the best decision was to kill him first.

Almost as soon as Cartwright stepped out to confront the gunman, Deep Water spotted the longhair moving upwards over the large rocky outcrop like an insect. He didn't wait to consider the options, but sprang from behind his cover and skipped across the broken boulders, heading away from Cartwright's destiny and towards his own.

He moved with all the agility of a mountain goat, his footing assured and confident, never pausing, drawn towards his quarry as if controlled by invincible strings, or a force beyond his understanding. His feet barely touched the ground and he only came to a stop when he was within spitting distance of the sharpshooter. Flattened full length, cheek against the stock of his rifle, the longhair aimed with such precision and concentration he appeared to have no awareness of the Indian's approach.

Until Deep Water spoke. "You die now."

Startled, the sharpshooter jerked his head around to face the Indian, and groaned in disbelief through his broken mouth.

Levelling the carbine towards the sharpshooter, Deep Water fought to control his rage. After so long, so much endeavor, such patience – to be here, in front of the destroyer of everything he held precious, his entire body trembled with the realization of it all. But this was not how he wanted it. To shoot this man with the carbine. No, it had to be personal, and massive. He hurled away his gun, swept out the broad-bladed knife he always kept at his side, and leaped forward, a fearsome war cry springing from his lips.

Talpas, keeping himself tight to the ground, swung his rifle around and fired. The heavy caliber bullet slammed into the Indian's torso. Despite being in mid-air, the impact was so great it sent him flying backwards, across the rocks to disappear down the side over which he had moments earlier climbed. The boom of the retort echoed through the gully and Talpas gazed at where the Indian had stood, not daring to believe the threat had passed. He blew out a breath and hastily took to reloading his rifle, not wanting to take anything for granted. If the Indian was dead, then all to the good, but if he wasn't, Talpas needed to be ready.

* * *

The hammers fell with a dull, metallic click. Blinking, Lol tried again, with the same result. Both guns were empty. This couldn't be happening and his head came up and he saw the man standing there, grinning. *Grinning*! "Oh, you sorry son of a bitch!"

"I'd say that was you, you brain dead idiot. I counted your shots as you came out of your hiding place, you dumb bastard. My name is Forrest Cartwright, Lieutenant in the Army of the United States, and I'm here to kill you, for what you did. What is your name, so I may inscribe it on your tombstone – if I have a mind to, of course."

"People call me Lol." He took in a deep breath and dropped both his guns. In his belt was Talpas' second Navy Colt. "If you aim to kill me, boy, best do it. I'm not convinced you can, however. But please try." And now it was Lol's turn to grin.

In that frozen moment in which desire for revenge, hatred and anger mingled with indecision, a single gunshot shattered the still air. Both Lol and Cartwright snapped their eyes upwards, both taken by surprise, but it was Lol, the more experienced, who reacted first and the Navy Colt came out from his belt in a blur, the hammer fully engaged. Cartwright gaped in disbelief and another grin spread across Lol's face, a face wet with sweat, but filled with triumph.

He squeezed the trigger and fired a single round.

Simms stopped, propping himself up with a single hand on a nearby rock, sucking in his breath, swallowing down the pain in his shoulder. He looked out across the land to where the two men stood, heard the first blast from a distant rifle and knew at once who the shooter was. Cursing, he strode forward, ignoring the pain of both his shoulder and scorching lungs, his breathing labored, the muscles in his legs like lead. Sweat blinding his vision, he knew what transpired before him nevertheless, and he also knew he would be too late to prevent any of it. He may well have averted the train robbery, but his ill-judged actions jeopardized the lives of his companions, men who were willing to do whatever they needed to do. Men driven by revenge, perhaps, but an overwhelming sense of duty. Brave men and now, quite probably, dead men.

He realized within half a dozen paces, he was too late. He saw the man ahead, the gun in his hand, and he watched Cartwright hitting the ground as the bullet struck home. A strangled moan of despair rattled in Simms throat and he sniffed loudly, putting the back of his gun hand against his nose. He moved across the remaining distance between himself and the young lieutenant's killer.

The gunman turned his head.

Their eyes met.

"Who in the hell are you?" asked the gunman. Not waiting for a reply, he whirled around in a half crouch, his Navy Colt coming up in a blur.

And Simms, steadfast, shot him – not once but many times, not stopping until his revolver was empty and the gunman was nothing but a mangled heap of shattered, bloodied flesh spread out across the ground.

Simms threw his revolver away and broke into a run to where Cartwright lay. The lieutenant's eyes were open, his mouth working soundlessly, and Simms fell on his knees next to him. Assessing the gaping wound in the young man's gut, Simms knew at once there was no chance of him surviving. Ripping away the bandana around his throat, Simms dabbed at the sweat across Cartwright's brow and forced a smile. "You just take it easy."

"I had him," Cartwright croaked, eyes fluttering, the light within them negligible, nothing but a tiny, feeble flame now. "Is he… Detective… is he…"

"Yes," said Simms, biting back his tears, "he's dead, Lieutenant. Gone to hell, where he belongs."

Something like peace spread across the young man's face, driving away all the tension, all the pain. "Thank you."

Simms managed a half-smile and brushed away sweat-drenched hair from the lieutenant's forehead. "It's over, now. You can rest."

"Rest. Yes. Yes, I can."

"You mustn't worry about anything, now Lieutenant, you just—"

"Tell my mother… Tell my mother I did all I could."

A sudden spasm gripped him and his body tensed, his eyes bulging. His hand flapped out in blind despair and Simms seized it, held it, and squeezed. But nothing came back in response, nothing except the awful collapse of all the young man's strength as life left him.

The silence stretched out and Simms remained sitting next to his young friend, continuing to hold onto his hand.

Straightening his back, Simms climbed to his feet, instinctively reaching for his shoulder, to knead it with his fingers whilst gazing down upon Cartwright's lifeless face, already grown waxy. He wondered, not for the first time, on the fragility of life, how it could so quickly be snuffed out. How many times had he stood and stared into the eyes of fallen comrades and how many times had he mused on the futility of it all. Nothing ever changed.

Without consciously wishing to, his thoughts turned to Cartwright's mother, and how he should break the news to her of her son's demise. The woman had already suffered so much but losing another loved one so close to the first, Simms feared her devastation would be total.

A bullet hit the ground next to where he had knelt, throwing up a tiny spurt of dust. Forcing all thoughts aside, he reacted as his years of training and experience dictated. He swept up Cartwright's revolver and sprinted towards a cluster of large rocks nearby, pressing himself behind them.

Damn it all. He cursed himself for allowing his concentration to wander because of course, the man who called himself Talpas lingered somewhere amongst the soaring rocks ahead. The first shot Simms had heard must have come from the sharpshooter's gun, but for whom was that bullet meant?

The answer proved obvious. Deep Water.

Simms checked Cartwright's revolver and cursed again. Having no powder or ball in his possession, all that remained were the three shots in the cylinder, with another four in the short-barreled Navy strapped to his ankle, giving a total of seven.

Another calculation rattled through his brain, estimating the time it would take the experienced Talpas to reload his rifle. A good, well-trained man, even under combat conditions, would take less than a minute, so Simms heaved himself up and broke cover. Head down, he bolted for the next closest group of boulders and slammed himself down amongst them. Resting with his back to the rock, he counted out the seconds, knowing there was precious little time left for him to make the foot of the rock. If he could, Talpas wouldn't be able to shoot due to the acuteness of the angle. So he stood, taking his chance, and the bullet hit him high up on the shoulder, sending him spinning to the dirt. On the impact, his revolver sprang from weakened fingers and skidded out of reach. He put his head back and took several deep breaths, knowing any hope of using the weapon was gone. Blood seeped from his shoulder, the same damned shoulder bruised and dislocated from the two tumbles he'd taken. Maybe it was a good thing, to have his injured limb blown totally out of commission, for at least he still retained the use of one good arm.

Gritting his teeth, he slithered over to yet another group of rocks and managed to get behind them. Here he lay, eyes screwed up, wheezing through the pain.

And then he heard it.

Another person's breathing and the slow, inexorable tread of feet coming ever closer.

A chuckle. Maniacal almost. The sound of victory, elated, assured. "Come on out, you bastard, or I'll come over and put a bullet in your pan."

Closing his eyes, Simms thought of the gun at his ankle. But to take it, with only one hand, in the confines of the space in which he lay… yet another hopeless idea.

"I ain't gonna ask you again."

So this was it, the moment, the time. Death had come a-callin' and everything he'd done, the thwarting of the train robbery, the capturing of Fergusson, Noreen waiting for him back at his fledgling ranch, all of it as dust. He sighed, not experiencing fear but rather a deep sadness. And regret. So much regret. Placing his one good palm into the ground, he levered himself up.

Bullets rang out, and instinct taking over, Simms flattened himself back against the rocks. But the bullets were not from Talpas' gun. Could they be from Deep Water? Elated almost, Simms chanced a look and saw Talpas retreating over the rocks, as agile as a cat. Tearing the pocket-sized Navy from its strapping on his ankle, Simms loosed off three quick shots. Talpas stopped, threw up his hands and fell.

A voice came to the detective, anxious, full of concern. The brakeman. "Good God almighty, Detective," said Bill, breathing laboured, "I felt sure you was done for!"

Simms wanted to throw his arms around this savior of his, but his shoulder pulsed with blood and pain and he sat down on top of the rock, which had been his cover, and managed a grim smile. "I'm only just alive, Bill, but thank God you came when you did."

"I think you might have winged him," said Bill. "I'll go check."

"Be careful," said Simms to the brakeman as he hurried off in pursuit.

Simms sat and stared at the ground, lost in thought. Of Cartwright, Noreen, of how close the end had been. He felt numb, from shock, pain, and misery. What had any of it been for?

Time passed and he knew nothing of it until the brakeman returned, muttering curses. "He got away. There were spots of blood on the ground and I followed 'em. But he made it to his horse and has galloped off."

"The Indian? Did you see him?"

"Indian? No sir, I didn't see anyone else, but God Almighty you have enough bodies here to open up your own private cemetery."

"And Fergusson?"

"Oh, he's all right. I have him well trussed up back in the caboose. Len the driver has a shotgun on him. Say, are you okay, Detective? You look mighty sickly. I think that shoulder of yours needs attending to."

"Yes," said Simms, "I think maybe it does."

And then he felt himself slipping into a gaping black hole and he didn't have the strength to stop himself from falling inside.

Twenty six

A month later

Simms stepped out of the church and stopped on the steps, considering the little group of grieving people standing in a tight knot a few paces away. A tall woman, dabbing her face with a white kerchief, nodding, forcing smiles to those close by, a woman Simms assumed was Cartwright's mother. He swallowed hard. Sitting at the back of the church, he'd listened to the eulogy, as well as the gut-wrenching sobs, and tried his best not to dwell on the events of the past weeks. His mission had been to thwart a train robbery, apprehend the culprits. His orders said nothing about watching a young man die in front of his eyes. Lieutenant Cartwright had been headstrong, gruff, inexperienced – naive even, but by God, his bravery stood head and shoulders above anything else anyone wished to level at him. Simms knew a lot about bravery, had seen many good men die in the war against Mexico over ten years before. Good men, young, with everything to live for. Cartwright was the same. A life snuffed out too soon, and for what? The man responsible for killing the young man's father may also be dead, but the sharpshooter continued to roam free. Simms may have shot him, but the bullet was not the one to have killed him.

And now this.

What to say to a grieving mother, what words of comfort could ever fill the void of first a husband, then a son lost to her?

Someone's fingers gripped his arm and he turned to see the preacher giving him a knowing smile. "It was good of you to come, Detective Simms. The family appreciated it."

"You think so?"

"I know so." A warm smile formed over his mouth and he eased Simms away, taking him out of earshot of the collection of mourners, perhaps fifteen or so in number, who muttered and mumbled to themselves in deferential tones not far off. "He was a brave man, the young Lieutenant. One of the killers, so I understand, is still free?"

"I will do my best to apprehend him," said Simms, but to give some explanation to his rather vague assurances, he raised his heavily bandaged arm slightly. "The doctors say I should be able to use my arm again in six weeks or so. Once I'm fully recovered, I intend to hunt the bastard down and—" He stopped abruptly, aware of his use of a profanity, and face heating up, looked away. "Sorry, I didn't mean to—"

"It's perfectly understandable, Detective. But I was not fishing for news over what you intend to do, rather what any of us can do to be safe in this wild land. It seems to me that almost every week I'm saying words of comfort over someone killed – murdered by either a villain or a savage. I'm not sure if my attempts at such comfort are best-placed. Will there ever be a time when we will know peace? Such men as shot the poor Lieutenant, and that other, a regulator so I have heard him called, are nothing more than brutalized, thoughtless killers. We owe so much to the likes of you, Detective, in doing your utmost to rid our land of such Godless sinners."

"Is that how you see them? Godless?"

"What else? They have been touched by Satan himself, whilst you, Detective Simms, are the Avenging Angel, the instrument of God Himself."

"I just do my job, is all." He twisted up his mouth and took a glance to his bandaged arm, "And not always so good either."

"Nonsense. You did everything you could. And when you have that man behind bars, we shall all come and enjoy seeing him dangle from the end of a rope. For that, I am certain, is where his destiny lies."

"You ever seen a man hang, Father?"

The preacher blinked. "I'm not sure I understand your question."

"No, well, never mind... You will, if you ever see it." He nodded and moved away, not wishing to listen to the man any longer. Any faith Simms bore left him years ago in the killing grounds of the Mexican War. He had no intention of re-igniting it.

As he went to walk across to where his horse stood, a figure stepped in front of him.

Mrs. Cartwright stood for a moment, before seizing hold of his lapels, and pressing her face against his coat, she wept. Simms didn't know what to do, or say, so he stood and allowed her to soak his jacket with her tears. And when some kind soul gently moved her away, he stood and watched and wondered if he might have done more. Jumping from the train, such a stupid thing to have done, exacerbating the previous injury to his shoulder. All of it so unnecessary. An ill-thought action, which lost so much precious time, costing the lives of Cartwright, and perhaps Deep Water too. The scout's body, like that of Talpas, had disappeared, but Simms felt certain it was out there, cold and alone in the vastness of the prairie.

Later, having left his horse at a livery stable, he took a cab to the offices of the Agency, finding solace in the hustle of the busy streets, the clamor of so many people, so many carriages clattering by. Chicago offered him the chance to escape, to become anonymous in the press of the passers-by. Perhaps he should remain here, take a desk job, learn to fill out reports and memoranda.

He sat down opposite Chesterton and studied his superior preparing two slim cigars, snipping off the ends before passing one across to Simms, who lit it with the proffered match in Chesterton's hand.

"Mr. Pinkerton is mighty impressed with what you did, Simms."

"I failed, and you know it."

"No, I wouldn't put it quite like that." Chesterton studied the glowing tip of his cigar. "You broke Fergusson's attempts at embezzling company funds, and saved the railroad company from financial disaster. I'd say that was pretty damned good myself."

"Cartwright died."

"Yes, well… No one is blaming you for that. In such circumstances, there are always bound to be casualties."

"That knowledge is sure gonna make me sleep real easy at night."

"Simms," Chesterton blew out a stream of smoke, "you have nothing to hold yourself guilty over. You performed your duty with admirable alacrity, and it must be said, professionalism. Despite your somewhat outrageous actions in this office the last time you were here, I've recommended you for promotion, Detective and I'm going to—"

"*Promotion?*" Simms leaned forward and stubbed out his barely touched cigar with a series of violent stabs in the ashtray sitting between the two men. "You have to be out of your mind if you think I'm going to accept that. I have no wish to give orders, or ask any man to do something which I myself could just as easily do."

"Which is why I'm giving you command of the Agencies first provincial office outside of Chicago."

"You're doing *what?*"

"I can't say I agree with your methods, Simms, and pulling a gun on the Director was not the most intelligent thing you have ever done…"

"He pulled a gun on me. I wasn't to know—"

"Which is exactly how I explained it to him after you had left. However, he took a lot of persuading not to fire your ass, Simms. So, a touch more humility might be in order."

"You're telling me I should be grateful, is that it? Grateful to carry out a job that sees a young man ruthlessly gunned down and myself receiving an injury that will put me out of action for the best part of two months? Yeah, I'm so very grateful."

"Either way you look at it, Simms, you're still in the employment of the Pinkerton Detective Agency, but now with further responsibilities."

"Heading an office?" Chesterton nodded, drawing on his cigar. "Well, it's not a million miles away from what I have been hoping for, so… Where is it?"

"Close to your adopted home, Simms. You're going to be the Pinkerton representative in Bovey. What do you think of that?"

But Simms didn't know what to think. As if hit by a punch between the eyes he sat and stared and barely felt anything at all, except for a numbness spreading across his chest and into his arms.

Twenty seven

Another two months

The weather was changing and the wind howled as the door to the store opened and a large man dressed in buckskin came through. Shivering, he placed the long barreled rifle in the corner and stretched out his arms before sitting down. He rubbed his hands, blew on them and rolled his shoulders. The man opposite; small, wiry and older than any other fixture in the building, frowned and stood up. He waddled over to the counter and pummeled it with his fist.

"Martinson," he shouted, "Martinson, you got yourself a customer."

Turning, the little man leaned back against the counter and studied the stranger for some time before speaking. "Are you the regulator?"

The stranger tossed his long hair and shrugged. "And what might one of them be?"

"We heard the silver mine over near Norwich Gulch was looking to hire some sharpshooters, as they'd been having problems with the Redskins. Thought you might be one of 'em."

"Redskin? Do I look like a Redskin?" The stranger grinned, throwing up a hand. "I'm joking, old-timer. I am a regulator, yes indeed I am."

Before the little man could continue, Martinson came through from the back, took one look at the stranger sitting at his table, and pulled up short.

"This is the regulator we've been expecting," said the little old man.

"Talpas," breathed Martinson, lowering his eyes to a place hidden underneath his counter.

The big man with the long hair grinned and leaned back, his coat falling open to reveal two ivory-handled Navy Colts in his belt. "I wouldn't make a play for that shotgun if I were you," he said, "I might take it personal."

Martinson's eyes grew wide. He took a deep breath. "What do you want?"

"A bowl of hot stew, one or two drinks, and…" He leaned right back with his chair so that it fell against the wall behind him. "Where I can find Detective Simms."

"Ah, him—" began the little old man, but Martinson shot out his hand and gripped him by the forearm before another word could be spoken. They exchanged a sharp look before the old man tore his arm free. "What the hell's the matter with you?"

"Just leave this to me," said Martinson.

"Oh, I think we can let our friend speak, can't we, Mister…?"

"People call me Foldin'. My friends call me Hank."

"Well, *Hank*, maybe you could point me in the right direction of the good detective's place. I'm kind of anxious to meet up with him again, seeing as we shared some moments out on the trail. We have much to discuss."

"Hank," said Martinson quickly, "I'm asking you, leave this to me."

"I think it might be best if you kept quiet, friend, and let Hank tell me the whereabouts of the good Detective Simms."

And when Martinson looked across to the big stranger, eyeing him as he sat so arrogantly and with such contempt, he realized there was no stepping back from this. So he acquiesced and Hank told the stranger where Simms lived. And after he'd gone, belly full of beef stew and hot coffee, Hank turned to Martinson, whose face was drained of color, and muttered, "I have the feeling I may have made a mistake."

Martinson shook his head, a sadness moving over him, and he said, "For one of them you have." Then he told Hank to look after the shop, went out back to his horse, and rode across the plain towards Simms, to tell his friend what was heading towards him.

Twenty eight

Fates conspired

After he'd spoken to the long-haired man and studied his quiet, almost lethargic withdrawal, Simms turned to Noreen standing in the doorway, took her by the arm and pressed her close, kissing her tenderly on the lips.

"I feel cold," she said.

"I want you to get back inside, bar the door and do not let anyone in. You hear me?"

"You're frightening me with this kind of talk."

"You've been through dangers before. This is no different. You keep away from the windows and the door. Sit in the far corner of the bedroom and listen out for my return."

Taking her in his arms, he held her for a long time, pressing his cheek against the top of her head. The swell of her belly brought a warmth to him and, for one glorious moment, it was as if no dangers existed and the world was good and secure.

But it wasn't.

He pushed her away and forced a smile. "Fetch me my carbine, then do as I say. Try not to worry."

"Easier said than done."

"I know."

She released a sigh and went back inside the cabin. Simms followed and pressed the door closed behind him. When she came out of the bedroom with his carbine in her hands, her face was downcast. "I have a bad feeling about this," she said.

"Please don't."

"Who is he?"

"He's a regulator – a hired killer. He goes by the name of Beaudelaire Talpas, although I now know that his real name is Ishmael Farage. He changed his identify with that of the real Talpas, whom he murdered some while back."

"Why did he do that?"

"To throw anyone off his scent. As I say, he's a killer. He was part of a team of train robbers, all of whom are now either dead or behind bars. He's the last one. And he's the most dangerous, due to that long-rifle he has slung over his back. I need to get close to him. So, I'll ride out, follow his trail as best I can, outflank him."

"But how will you know where he's going? You've often said you're not a scout. What if you lose the trail? What if he—"

Without a word, he pulled her close again. Since he'd returned with her and they had shared this comfortable home together, his feelings had developed far deeper than he could ever have imagined. Often, in the middle of the night, when he would sit bolt upright in the dark, the demons of a violent past coming to haunt him once more, she was there, to hold him and comfort him. Such nights seldom came now, replaced by dreams of a lighter kind. When she took to being sick and the doctor examined her, the news he brought changed Simms entire way of thinking. Noreen was pregnant. Before the year was out, so the doctor said, they would be proud parents.

He kissed the top of her head. "It's going to be fine," he said. "Once I've cornered him, I'll arrest him, take him in for trial. There'll be only one outcome – he'll be hanged, for everything he's done."

Lifting her head by the chin, he went to kiss her once more, but stopped – alert, eyes unblinking, listening.

"What is it?"

"A horse," he said, pulling out the revolver from his hip. "Stay here."

She stifled a yelp, clamping a hand over her mouth and stepped away. Simms gave her a reassuring nod, then slipped over to the door and eased it open. He breathed a long sigh and swung it open entirely.

Martinson jumped down from his horse, troubled, face drawn, eyes wide. "He's been here, hasn't he?"

Simms holstered his gun. "You saw him?"

"Talpas. Yes, he called at the store. Before I could say anything, old Hank Folding told him where you lived. I tried to outpace him, but Bart here is too old to keep up the pace. I'm sorry."

"No matter." Simms reached over and squeezed Martinson's arm. "I appreciate you coming here, but listen, I want you to go back, get a telegram off to Fort Bridger. Tell Johnstone Talpas is here and I'm bringing him in."

"You? But… Jeez, Simms, your arm is barely out of its sling. What if he—"

"My arm is fine," said the detective, and as if to prove it, he raised the previously injured limb and swung it over in a wide arc. He smiled. "See, nothing at all. Besides, I plan to take him by surprise and creep up close. He'll have no chance to use that damned buffalo gun of his."

"You want me to take Noreen back to town? It might be safer."

Giving this suggestion a moment's thought, Simms glanced over to the open doorway of his ranch house, with Noreen standing there. Her smile swept away all his concerns. "No, she'll be fine. Now, get going, and thanks again."

Martinson touched his hat with a forefinger, turned and swung himself back into his saddle. He kicked old Bart in the flanks and the tired horse broke into something of a faltering canter. Simms went up to Noreen and stroked her cheek.

"Remember, bar the door. Get in the bedroom…"

"I know. Keep away from the windows." She reached down behind the door and came back with his carbine. He took it, checked it was loaded, and kissed her lightly on the nose. "I won't be long."

She closed the door and, as he made his way to the rear and the small paddock where his horse was tethered, he heard the unmistakable heavy clunk of the bar dropping across the door. Grunting with satisfaction, he stepped into the barn, hefted the saddle, which hung over a stall rail, and froze.

Cursing himself, he closed his eyes for a moment as the shadow fell across the open door. Simms, the enormity of the situation pressing over him, could do nothing but wait.

Behind him, the voice came low, its tone mocking. "Well, Detective, the plan was to get close, huh? Seems like you succeeded, so why don't you just unhitch your gun belt and drop everything to the ground. And *slowly*, Detective, or this big old buffalo gun as you called it will blow you apart before you can spit."

Letting out a deep sigh, Simms allowed his shoulders to drop and did as ordered. The carbine went first, then the Navy in its shoulder holster, followed finally by the big Colt Dragoon. Raising his hands, he turned and squinted towards the opening.

"Step outside," said Talpas, gesturing with the rifle, moving away to ensure enough distance remained between them to make any attempted attack impossible.

Outside again, Simms stood, breathing as shallowly as he could, not wishing to give the regulator the satisfaction of seeing his despair.

"I could have shot you as you stood there, out in the open, teaching your pretty little girl how to fire that big old Colt of yours."

"Why didn't you."

"Because I want to see the fear in your eyes, Detective, when I squeeze this trigger. I want to glory in that flicker of total defeat, the realization that death is the only outcome – *your* death."

"Then just do it, you bastard."

Talpas chuckled. "Oh, I will, but first I need to humiliate you just a touch more. Get on your knees."

Simms directed his attention on the muzzle of the rifle in the man's hands. At this distance, a bullet anywhere in his body would be lethal. There was no other choice so he dropped down on his knees, resting his hands on his head. His eyes grew moist at the thought of Noreen and their unborn child, a child he would never see. Not now, due to his own stupidity.

"There's something you should know," said Simms, as he noted the man's finger squeezing the rifle trigger.

"Oh? And what do I need to know, Detective? Want to give me a confession, say you're sorry, beg me for mercy?"

"No. Nothing like that. I know who you are. Ishmael Farage."

For a moment, a shadow of indecision crossed the regulator's face and he frowned. "That's interesting. How did you find out?"

"A good friend, someone who served with you, told me. The Agency will track you down, Farage, and they won't rest until you're dangling from the end of a rope."

A snigger followed by a dismissive shake of the head. "They'll never find me, Detective. As soon as you're in the dirt, I'll make my way to Missouri, lose myself in the badlands. Why, I might even change my identity again."

"They'll still find you."

"No, they won't. They'll forget." A grin spread across his face. "But before I do take my leave, I might just go and pay your little lady a visit. She's a pretty one, Detective. You've done mighty well for yourself. A woman like that, a nice ranch, future looking bright. Until you made your play against me, you dumb sonofabitch. You should've made sure your bullet put me down for good."

"Yes. I should have."

"Still, no point in dwelling on past mistakes. Give up a little prayer, Detective. Time to die."

Talpas settled himself again, putting his cheek alongside the stock of the rifle and took careful aim.

Simms closed his eyes and gave up that silent prayer.

Twenty nine

The trail to death

In the hard-baked earth, with his face flat in the dirt, he thought he heard his father's voice, shouting to him from across the prairie. Ignoring the pain, he lifted his head and turned and there his father was, sitting astride his piebald pony, a hunting bow in one hand, the other raised in greeting.

"Pick yourself up, my son, and follow me."

So Deep Water did. He pushed down with his palms and got to his knees. The bullet had skimmed across his shoulder, leaving a deep furrow in the flesh. The bullet, however, had not struck home. The wound burned with an intensity he would never have believed possible, but he lived, and more importantly, the blood seeping from his damaged flesh coagulated, growing crusty.

"You are alive, my son, and you have much to do."

As if in a daze, Deep Water went over to where he'd hobbled his own pony, jumped onto its back, and gently eased it in behind his father and together they rode out towards the setting sun.

In the morning, when he woke, his father was no longer there. No sign of him remained and Deep Water, with the truth coming to him with the ferocity of the most vicious of enemies, broke down and wept. The spirit of his father may well have appeared to him, to give him the strength and the courage to move, but the realization that his father was no more was almost too much to bear. So he sat and he wept and he did not get up on his horse again for many, many hours.

He roamed the land for the next few days, surviving on whatever roots and small game he could find. At one point, he came across three wagons, the occupants dead, arrows piercing their hearts, everything stripped bare from their bodies. In the back of one wagon, underneath the bodies of the women, he found a bag of grain, which he gave to his horse, and he slept on the ground, between the wheels, whilst the sun raged overhead.

Time passed, the days merging into one elongated stretch of confusion and despair. He caught a glimpse of a hunting party, silhouetted against the sky, a long line of bent over warriors, ravaged by hunger and cold. Perhaps they were more Shoshone, continuing their hunt for the hated regulator, so Deep Water shadowed them.

On the fourth day, he received his reward and watched the gunfight played out far below in the valley. Warriors fell, and during a lull, a lone rider galloped off.

The hunt continued, punctuated with the single shot of a rifle and the death of another warrior. No matter how hard they rode, the Shoshone could not get close with the killer, but their burning desire for revenge drove them on, each companion's death stoking the fire. Keeping far enough away to remain unnoticed, Deep Water saw it all and his spirit sank ever deeper with each new killing.

Perhaps weeks later, passing into months, he came into Fort Bridger and reported to Colonel Johnstone, who studied him with livid eyes and informed him of Fergusson's arrest at the hands of Simms. Deep Water's joy boiled over, and he cried out with relief. But the Colonel merely snarled, "He almost died, whilst you… Where the hell were you?"

"Talpas shot me, but I recovered. I have tracked him."

"Have you found him?"

"I lost the trail."

"Damn your hide. Did you know Cartwright died? And Simms required surgery on his arm? Damn it, he almost lost the use of it."

"There was nothing I could have done."

"Well," Johnstone stomped around inside the command tent, "that's as maybe, but we have a barrel load of shit emptying all over our heads. The Mormons have ambushed a patrol out near the Colorado River. A messenger managed to get back here with the news and I'm sending a troop over there to find the perpetrators. You can help with the tracking."

It took some time, but Deep Water led the soldiers to where the Mormons were camped. He sat astride his horse and watched, impassive, not caring for anything very much anymore, as soldiers and Mormons exchanged gunfire. If any died, he neither knew nor cared. All his thoughts were with Talpas and what the man might be planning next. So, when it was over and his duty fulfilled, he rode away towards Simms's ranch. If he knew anything about Talpas, it was the man's utter ruthlessness. Such a man could not allow Simms to live. So he rode and the trail, when he found it, led straight to the Pinkerton's home.

He should have felt elation. A sense of triumph. Instead, there was nothing. Only the deep, mournful realization that this was what his life had become – the all-consuming need to kill, to avenge the death of his family. In the process, a blackness gripped his soul, the bitter, destructive power of hate changing him, making him less than human. When he tied up his pony at a nearby tree and scrambled over the rise, he saw him. Talpas. And someone else too.

Simms.

Deep Water checked his revolver, eased his knife a few times in and out of its scabbard, then slithered across the ground, making his slow, deliberate way towards the ranch house.

Those seconds were like an eternity. Simms drew in a deep breath, forcing his mind to remain blank. The bullet would strike and snuff out his life before he heard the retort of the blast. Any moment now.

The first inkling he had that the outcome might be very much different from what he expected, was the sudden pounding of feet across the ground. He sprang open his eyes to see Deep Water charging with his knife held aloft, a war cry screeching from his open mouth. And Talpas, swiveling from his hips, dropping the rifle to his waist, firing a snap shot towards the fast approaching scout. The bullet, ill-aimed, went wide and Deep Water rammed into the regulator, the pair of them smacking onto the earth, screaming, rolling, kicking, both desperate to find leverage. Talpas managed to get his hand around the scout's wrist, preventing the downward strike of the knife. But Deep Water was strong and he wriggled and writhed, breaking free of the grip. At the same moment, however, Talpas cracked his fist across the scout's jaw, a short snap of a punch, but enough to throw Deep Water away from him.

Scrambling to his feet, Talpas slammed his foot into Deep Water's ribs. Howling, the scout spun away, only to receive another kick in the face, so powerful it almost tore his head from his neck and he fell backwards, spread-eagled across the ground, the knife falling from his weakened grip.

Stepping back, Talpas – winded, blowing hard, took a moment and went to pull out one of the Navy's at his waist.

Simms, having watched it all, sat back on his backside, ripped up his trouser leg and drew the Pocket Navy from the ankle holster. The Pocket Navy he had viewed with such disdain when Pinkerton first made him a gift of it. Four shots. He didn't need any more.

He put his teeth together and whistled.

Talpas turned.

Their eyes met.

And Simms shot him four times in the chest.

They stood together in front of their house, Simms with his arm around Noreen, both watching in silence as Deep Water secured the body across the back of the mule Simms had supplied.

"Thank you," said Noreen as Deep Water swung up onto his horse.

He nodded but did not speak, allowing only the briefest of smiles to flutter across his lips. Then he turned his horse away and set off across the plain.

After a few moments, Noreen said, "What will he do?"

"After he delivers the body and claims the reward, who knows. I'm not sure even he knows. He's been after that bastard for so long, I don't think he knows anything else."

"And you? What will you do?"

Frowning, Simms looked down at her for a long time, until he finally smiled. "Why, look after you, of course." He kissed her. "And that baby of ours."

With the sun dropping below the backdrop of distant mountains, he led her inside their ranch house. This time, he didn't bar the door.

THE END

Dear reader,

We hope you enjoyed reading *In The Blood*. Please take a moment to leave a review, even if it's a short one. Your opinion is important to us.

Discover more books by Stuart G. Yates at https://www.nextchapter.pub/authors/stuart-g-yates

Want to know when one of our books is free or discounted for Kindle? Join the newsletter at http://eepurl.com/bqqB3H

Best regards,

Stuart G. Yates and the Next Chapter Team

The story continues in:
To Die in Glory by Stuart G. Yates

To read the first chapter for free, head to:
https://www.nextchapter.pub/books/to-die-in-glory

About the Author

Stuart G Yates is the author of an eclectic mix of books, ranging from historical fiction through to contemporary thrillers. Hailing from Merseyside, he now lives in southern Spain, where he teaches history, but dreams of living on a narrowboat in Shropshire, or perhaps somewhere more exotic, like the Philippines.

Dear reader,

Thank you for taking time to read *In The Blood*. If you enjoyed it, please consider telling your friends or posting a short review. Word of mouth is an author's best friend and much appreciated.

Lightning Source UK Ltd.
Milton Keynes UK
UKHW040633301221
396391UK00001B/56